"I'll be there to cheer you on, Sam. I promise."

"Thank you, Laci," Eric said softly.

"I wouldn't miss it."

"Okay! See you Tuesday," Sam said before running off to join several other children.

Laci looked up to see Eric's gaze on her. "I hope he isn't bothering you. I'm at a complete loss here. Sam has never taken to anyone the way he has you."

"Well, I've never met up with anyone quite like Sam either. He's a special little boy."

Eric cleared his throat. "I certainly think so."

"Eric, please don't worry. Sam is not bothering me. I'm honored that he seems to like me." And she spoke the truth. It wasn't Sam who bothered her. It was his dad. He kept turning up in her dreams at night. . .and in the middle of the day, too.

JANET LEE BARTON and her husband, Dan, have recently moved to Oklahoma and feel blessed to have at least one daughter and her family living nearby. Janet loves being able to share her faith and love of the Lord through her writing. She's very happy that the kind of romances the Lord has called her to write can be read by and shared with women of all ages.

Books by Janet Lee Barton

HEARTSONG PRESENTS

Family
Reunion

Janet Lee Barton

Heartsong Presents

To my Lord and Savior for showing me the way and to the family He has blessed me with. I love you all.

A note from the Author:
I love to hear from my readers! You may correspond with me by writing:

Janet Lee Barton
Author Relations
PO Box 721
Uhrichsville, OH 44683

ISBN 978-1-59789-445-6

FAMILY REUNION

All scripture quotations are taken from the King James Version of the Bible.

All of the characters and events in this book are fictitious. Any resemblance to actual persons, living or dead, or to actual events is purely coincidental.

Our mission is to publish and distribute inspirational products offering exceptional value and biblical encouragement to the masses.

PRINTED IN THE U.S.A.

one

Laci Tanner sighed as she looked over the books of her interior design business, Little Touches. She was in the black, but just barely. That's where she seemed to stay. Since opening her shop she'd struggled—first to get those books out of the red and then to keep them in the black. She wondered if it would ever get better.

She'd thought moving from her small hometown of Sweet Springs, New Mexico, to Dallas, Texas, would be the way to go in starting up a business. But the past several years of struggling to get her company up and running had left her little time to have a real life in Dallas or anywhere else. She wanted more from living than working twelve-hour days and eating takeout. And lately she'd been feeling a little lonely and a whole lot homesick.

She'd never imagined how hard it would be to compete with the larger companies in Dallas, although her family had warned her. She'd figured they were just trying to get her to change her mind about moving there, but it seemed they knew what they were talking about.

In the last few months, she'd been debating about whether or not to leave Texas and set up her business in a smaller town. . .even thinking about returning to Sweet Springs. But it was hard to admit her dream hadn't lived up to her expectations.

Lost in her memories of the grand dreams she'd woven about owning her own business, it took her a minute to realize her telephone was ringing. She picked up the receiver on the third ring. "Hello?"

"Laci, it's Mom."

As if she couldn't recognize her own mother's voice. But there was something in her tone. "Mom, what's wrong?"

"Your grandmother has had a stroke, dear, and—"

"Oh, Mom—Gram? How is she?"

"Honey, we don't know yet. But I thought you might want to come home—"

Laci swallowed a sob and pressed her fingers against her tear-filled eyes, knowing that if her mom heard her cry they'd both be bawling over the phone line. "Yes, of course I do. Are you all right?"

"I'm worried."

Those two words were all it took for Laci to know what she had to do. "I'll be there tomorrow, okay?"

"Okay. Are you going to drive or fly?"

Laci looked at the clock. It was nine o'clock at night. She couldn't get a flight out until the morning anyway, and someone would have to meet her in Las Cruces and then drive back to Sweet Springs. She wouldn't get there any faster by flying. "I'll drive."

"Please be careful, dear."

"I will, Mom. I love you. Have Daddy"—Laci's voice broke, and she paused before continuing—"give you a hug for me."

She could tell her mother was having a hard time talking, too. "I will, dear. I love you, too. And, Laci?"

"Yes, Mom?"

"Please pray."

Laci nodded even though her mother couldn't see her. "I will."

She hung up the receiver and released the sob she'd been

holding back. *Gram. A stroke.* Laci shook her head and wiped at the tears that streamed out of her eyes. She didn't have time to cry—she had too much to do before she left. But that didn't stem the tears as she went about making a list of all she had to do: call Myra Branson, her assistant manager; pack for a long visit because she didn't know how long or short her visit might be; fill the car.

In between each item, she prayed the same prayer over and over. "Oh, please, dear Lord, let Gram be all right. Please be with Mom, too."

Laci began packing her bags while she called Myra to let her know she was going home. She tried to remember all the things that would need her immediate attention. "There's that shipment coming in on Thursday, and the Wilkinsons' drapes will be ready on Friday. And—"

"Don't worry about anything, Laci. I'll call you if there is a problem. Just get home to your family," Myra said.

"You're right. I know you'll be able to handle anything that comes up." And she would. Myra was very capable, and Laci knew she was leaving her business in good hands. Besides, she was only an e-mail or cell phone call away. None of it mattered at the moment anyway. She had to get to Gram and to her mother.

Laci had trouble sleeping that night, but it wasn't worry about her business that kept her awake. It was anger at herself for not making it to the last family reunion. Gram had wanted her to come so badly. But it had been right after she opened her business in Dallas, and at the time she felt she couldn't get away. To her way of thinking, nothing was more important than getting Little Touches up and running.

She threw her covers off and walked over to the window. How could she have thought any of that was more important than her family? She swiped at a lone tear that trailed down her cheek. What if Gram didn't make it? Laci felt the moan rise in her chest before she ever heard it escape. *Oh, please, dear Lord. Let Gram recover. Please let her be all right.*

❧

Eric Mitchell dropped Sam, his five-year-old son, at preschool and headed toward his office on Main Street. But his rumbling stomach wouldn't be ignored. He'd fed Sam a breakfast of cereal and orange juice but had been so busy getting a rumpled shirt out of the dryer and ironing it for his son that he hadn't managed to eat anything himself. While Sam finished his breakfast, Eric had folded a load of towels he'd taken out of the dryer the night before, wondering if he would ever catch up around the house.

After he parked his car at the office, he gave in to his hunger pains and hurried down the block to Deana's Diner. He entered as John Tanner was leaving. Normally a very friendly person, John only nodded to Eric before he walked out the door. The mood inside the restaurant was more somber than Eric remembered, and he couldn't help but wonder at the cause.

He took his normal seat by the window and waited until Deana Russell, better known to everyone in town as Dee, brought him a menu and a cup of coffee. She looked about as solemn as John had.

"Dee? Is something wrong?" Normally Eric didn't pry into other people's business, but with John leaving so abruptly and Dee looking as if she were about to cry, he wanted to do something to help if he could.

She let out a huge sigh. "Ellie Breland had a stroke and is in the hospital. The family is very worried."

"Oh, no," Eric said. Ellie Breland was John's grandmother

and the grandmother of two of Eric's good friends, Jake and Luke Breland. Eric had spent a lot of time at her house when he was younger, and suddenly he felt as if he'd just received news that his own grandmother was in serious condition.

"What can I get you this morning?" Dee asked.

Eric shook his head. His appetite seemed to have disappeared. "Maybe just some toast and jelly."

Dee nodded as if she understood. "Coming right up."

Eric sipped his coffee and thought about the last time he'd seen Miss Ellie, as most everyone called her. He was going over the plans to the home he'd built for Jake and Sara before they married and while Jake was still living with his grandmother. When they'd finished looking over the plans, Miss Ellie insisted he join them for pie and coffee. Eric could almost taste that pie now. No one in Sweet Springs was more hospitable than Ellie Breland. She was a very sweet woman, and he prayed she would recover completely. His heart went out to her family, to John and especially to Jake and Luke— their grandmother had raised them. He was sure they were taking it hard. He probably ought to check on them.

"Here you go," Dee said, sounding a little more like herself as she set a plate of toast and jelly in front of him. "I'm used to seeing you and Sam for supper, but you usually only eat breakfast here on the weekends. Did you have a bad morning?"

"Just a busy one," Eric said. "I did manage to feed Sam, though."

"I never doubted that for a minute," Dee said. "You take real good care of him."

"Thanks, Dee. I try." Her comment meant more to him than she knew. It wasn't easy trying to be both dad and mom to his son since his wife, Joni, had passed away when Sam was only a few months old. He worried that Sam was missing what only a mother could give him, but he did the best he could to see that his little boy knew he was loved and cared for.

"He's an adorable little boy, Eric. Tell him hi for me."

"I will," Eric assured her as she waved and stepped away to take care of a couple of customers who sat down at the table next to him.

Sam liked Dee. She always talked to him and made him feel special. Maybe Eric would bring him back for supper tonight. He slathered jelly on his toast and bit into it, wondering why his buttered toast never quite tasted like it did here. It took only about ten minutes to finish his light breakfast. After leaving the money to cover his meal and a decent tip for Dee, he headed for his office. He'd call Jake or Luke a little later to see how their grandmother was doing.

ॐ

The trip home to Sweet Springs was a long, soul-searching one for Laci. She prayed her grandmother would be all right and that she would have a chance to tell her how much she loved her and how sorry she was she hadn't come home more often—especially for that reunion.

She owed her parents the same thing. They'd been the ones to visit her in Dallas, making frequent trips to make sure their "baby" was all right. Now she realized that's exactly what she'd been acting like the past few years—a baby, thinking more of herself than anyone else. She was always too busy. Too busy to call, too busy to take off a few days and make sure they were all right, and too busy to come to the last family reunion. Too selfish was what she'd been.

Now Laci was filled with remorse that she'd been so self-absorbed. Had she made the right decision to leave Sweet Springs? Looking back, Laci didn't think so. She'd been so young and full of herself—thinking that if she could just get out of her small town and into a city like Dallas she could make it big in the decorating world. Laci gave a delicate snort at the very thought of her audacity.

Well, that certainly hadn't happened. Laci sighed. *Nor was it likely to.* She managed to make a living for herself and pay Myra a decent wage, but that was about it. She could have done that in Sweet Springs. . .and been around family and friends. Instead, she was miles away from those she loved, and she wasn't getting ahead. If she were honest with herself, she would have to admit she was blessed just to be doing as well as she was.

What made her think she could compete in a city where she knew so few people? And yet Dallas was where she'd always wanted to go. Now she couldn't say why, but when she'd set off for Texas the city had seemed glamorous and exciting.

But the reality was that there was nothing glamorous or exciting about living in Dallas. Her life seemed to consist of working long hours and only going to church and the occasional movie or out to dinner with the few friends she'd managed to make. And still she'd stayed. Why? Because it was easier than admitting her family had been right and she'd been wrong.

As Laci topped Comanche Hill outside Roswell, New Mexico, excitement welled up inside her as she saw the town laid out below. She could see El Capitan Mountain off in the distance and knew she'd be home in just over an hour. Roswell was the largest town near Sweet Springs, and she and her family often shopped there. As she entered the city limits and traveled down Second Street to Main, she chuckled and shook her head at the alien displays. She might think it was silly, but the *Roswell Incident* had certainly done its part in helping the town's economy in the last few decades.

She enjoyed seeing all the changes down Second Street as she traveled straight through town and back out onto open highway. She loved the change of scenery from flat farmland around Roswell, up through the foothills of the Rocky Mountains. Apple orchards dotted the landscape around the Hondo River Valley as she neared Sweet Springs.

She passed the new mall, several motels, and restaurants on the highway before she turned off to enter the main part of town. Her mother had told her Sweet Springs was growing, and she was pleased to see how much it had.

But Laci wasn't prepared for the sense of homecoming she felt just driving down Main Street on the way to the hospital. She passed familiar tree-lined streets and the church her family attended. She spotted the law firm her brother John and cousin Jake shared, and she couldn't help but feel a spark of family pride. When she passed Deana's Diner, her mouth began to water at the thought of Dee's hamburgers and fries.

It wasn't until she pulled into the hospital parking lot that she felt sudden tears sting the back of her eyelids, and she didn't know if it was because she was home or because she was scared to go inside. She was afraid of what kind of news awaited her. She'd had a hard time getting a good signal on her cell phone on the way home. The one time she'd managed to get through to her mother, the line was filled with static. Laci wasn't sure her mom had been able to hear her when she told her she'd be going directly to the hospital to see how Gram was. Most probably that's where the whole family would be, but she wouldn't know until she got there.

She didn't bother to stop at the information desk; instead, she headed for the intensive care unit. She walked up to the nurses' station and told the nurse on duty who she was and asked if she could see her grandmother.

"She's no longer here," the nurse said, barely looking up at her.

Laci's heart seemed to stop, and she felt as if the breath had been knocked right out of her. But she forced out the words. "No longer here? I—"

"We just moved her. She's in room. . .204."

Laci couldn't contain the small sob of relief that escaped.

"Oh, dear, I'm sorry," the nurse said, finally looking at her. "I should have realized you'd think something else. She's doing much better. She's been moved to a private room and—"

"I—it's okay. She's in a room." Laci started to leave then realized she wasn't sure where the room was in relation to the nurses' station. She turned back to the nurse. "Where—"

"Come on. I'll take you to her." Her name tag read MARGE MONROE.

"Thank you, Marge," Laci said as the woman stepped out from behind the desk.

Marge led the way down the hall and around the corner before stopping next to room 204.

"I think some of your family are in there with her, but if you don't make too much noise it'll be all right." She smiled and turned to go.

Unsure of what shape her grandmother was in, Laci stood outside her room for a moment trying to gather courage to go in. She sent up a silent prayer of thanksgiving that Gram was out of intensive care. Surely that meant she was going to be all right.

But when she opened the door and peeked around it, nothing could have prepared her for what she saw. She knew others were in the room, but all she could see was the woman in the bed. The energetic woman she remembered looked frail and pale, but when she saw Laci her eyes shone bright and clear with recognition.

Laci rushed to her side.

"I'm glad. . .you made it," Gram said. Her speech was slow, and she seemed to be talking out of one side of her mouth, but Laci could only be thankful she could speak.

"I'm glad I did, too, Gram." Laci choked back a sob.

"Don't. . .you cry now. I'm. . .going to be all right." She reached out and grabbed Laci's hand.

Laci could only nod and give her grandmother's hand a gentle squeeze.

"But if I'd known. . .this would get you here, it would have been. . .worth it a long time ago."

"Mother!" Laci's mom said from behind her. But she joined the others in the room in a relieved chuckle.

Laci bent down and kissed her grandmother's cheek, happy to see she'd lost none of her feistiness. She felt her mother's hand on her shoulder, and when she turned she enveloped her in a hug.

"I hope you'll be able to stay awhile, dear. I—we all need you here."

Before she could answer her mother, her dad pulled her into a hug. "I'm so glad you came home, honey. We've sure missed you around here."

"I've missed you, too, Dad." More than she'd realized until that moment.

"It's good to see you, sis," John said as he gave her a bear hug and kissed her on the cheek. "I've really missed you."

Then her cousins Jake and Luke each took a turn welcoming her home.

"It's good to see you, Laci." Jake hugged her.

Then Luke pulled a lock of her hair as he'd loved to do

when they were kids. "You're looking good, Laci. It's about time you came home for a while." He hugged her, too. "Sure wish you'd think about staying."

Laci felt bad. She hadn't made it home for a long time. Not for Jake's wedding, not for Luke's—and not for the reunion. Nor had she kept up with much of what was happening with all of them. And yet here they were, welcoming her with open arms.

She didn't deserve this kind of homecoming. But she would cherish it always.

two

It wasn't long until Laci's grandmother told them all to go home for a while so she could get some rest.

"Let me stay awhile, Gram, please?" Laci asked.

"No. You just made. . .a long trip, and I know you are tired. You. . .can come back later for a little while."

"But—"

"No buts. Your. . .parents need to visit. . .with you."

"We'll come back later," Laci's dad said. "Your gram could use some rest."

"Okay."

"Let's go grab a bite to eat," her mother suggested. "I'm sure all you've done is fill up your car and grab a cup of coffee or a soft drink on your way here."

Her mother knew her too well. Laci grinned and nodded. "I guess I could use some food."

"Well, I'm going to take off," Jake said. "Sara tires pretty easily these days, and Meggie doesn't. I'd better go check on the two of them."

"Sara's not well?" Laci asked.

"The baby is due in a month or so, dear," her mother reminded her.

"Oh, that's right. Sara's all right, though? There aren't any problems with the baby?" Laci asked, trying not to show she'd forgotten Sara was expecting. But she wasn't even sure she ever knew. Surely she had. Her mother would have told her.

"She's fine." Jake grinned. "Or as fine as a woman can be

16

this far along in her pregnancy, so Gram tells me." He bent to kiss Gram's forehead. "I'll stop in later, Gram."

"Stay home. Sara needs you," Gram said slowly. "I'm going. . .to be fine. 'Sides, Will is going to. . .be here soon."

"I'm surprised he isn't here now."

"He said he had. . .something he had to do," Gram said. "Said he'd be back to. . .make sure I eat."

"Well, we'll check back, but I know Will would like a little time with you," Laci's mom said.

Laci exchanged a glance with her mother. Will? Could she mean Sara's grandfather? She opened her mouth to ask, but before she could get the words out, her mother placed her hand on her shoulder and propelled her toward the door.

"We'll check back a little later, Mom. We'll let the nurse know we'll be at the diner. If you need us—"

"Go," Gram said. She lifted her hand and gave a little wave. "Eat."

"All right," John said. "But you behave while we're gone, you hear?"

That brought a smile to Gram's face. "I'll try."

They filed out of the room and rode the elevator down to the lobby where they parted company with Jake and Luke.

"I'm going home, too," Luke said. "Rae wants to come back with me this evening."

"Sara does, too. Aunt Nora said she'd watch Meggie for us. I hope Gram will be able to go home soon," Jake said.

"I certainly hope so. I don't like this hospital stuff. I'll feel better knowing she's well enough to go home. I'd like to talk her into coming out to our house, but you know how she is," Laci's mom said.

"Lydia, she's going to be all right." Laci's dad put his arm around her mother.

"I know, Ben." She reached up and patted his hand. "I'll just feel better when the doctor releases her."

"Too bad Michael isn't a heart doctor," Jake said.

"Yes, it is. He knows how much better we'll all feel to get her home."

"Michael? That's Aunt Nora's husband, right?" Laci asked. "And Will is Sara's grandpa?"

"That's right."

Laci nodded. Much had happened in her family since she'd been gone, and Laci was glad she'd guessed right. "I thought so. And I take it that Gram and Will are kind of an item?"

"You could say that," her mother answered. "They've been seeing each other for several years now. We've all been expecting them to get married, but it hasn't happened yet."

They walked outside into the waning sunlight and piled into John's new SUV for the ride to the diner. From the backseat Laci could see yard signs and posters with her brother's name on them. She'd almost forgotten his campaign for the U.S. Senate was underway. Sisterly pride in John washed over her, followed by a crashing wave of disappointment in herself as she realized she hadn't even asked how the campaign was going in the last few months. Just when had she become so selfish?

"How are things looking for November?" she asked now, wondering if her brother thought her interest was a little late in coming.

But he didn't appear to be upset with her as he maneuvered the vehicle out of the parking lot. "It's going really well. Once we know Gram is truly all right, I'll be getting out on the road again."

"We were planning to go out with him this time," Laci's mom said. "But I'll have to be sure about Mother before I leave town."

"Don't worry about it, Mom," John said. "I wouldn't want her to be here alone."

"Maybe I can help," Laci found herself saying. "I can stay awhile if you all need me to."

"Are you sure, honey?" her dad asked.

And suddenly she was. She'd put the people she loved second to herself for way too long, and it was time that changed. "I'm sure."

"We'll see. I just can't leave Mother until I know she's well on the way to recovery."

Laci could see the strain of the past few days on her mother's face. She took hold of her hand and squeezed it. "I can understand that."

Tears welled up in her mother's eyes, and she squeezed Laci's hand. "I know you can."

They pulled up at the diner, and her mother brushed away her tears as Laci's dad opened the door for her. John had opened Laci's side, and she jumped out.

"Thanks for coming, sis," he said, draping his arm around her shoulders as they walked to the diner. "It means a lot to have you here. I think Mom has really needed you."

Laci nodded, fighting back a few tears of her own. "I'm glad I'm here."

As they entered, it seemed everyone in the diner looked at John expectantly.

"She's doing better," he said. "They've moved her to a private room."

At the cheers that erupted at his words, Laci was reminded of the wonderful things about a small town. Nearly everyone at the diner seemed to know about her grandmother and had most likely been praying for her.

Dee came from behind the counter to give her a hug. "It's

good to see you, girl. I've missed you."

Laci hugged her back. "I've missed you, too." Although she was a few years younger than Dee, they'd gone to school together, and Laci had been coming to the diner since back when Dee's mom ran it.

"I hope you are able to stay awhile. I think your family needs you right now," Dee whispered in her ear.

"I'm planning on it."

"Good." Dee turned to her mother and gave her a hug, too. "I'm so glad about your mother. I'll keep praying she recovers completely and quickly."

"Thank you, dear. Please do," Laci's mom said.

Dee gave them all menus and took their drink orders before punching John on the shoulder and turning away. Once, when they were younger, Laci had thought her brother and Dee would end up getting married. Obviously that hadn't happened, but still there was something about the way they looked at each other.

"I think Dee's been as worried as the rest of us," her dad said.

"From what I've heard, the whole town has been," John added. "And I think Dee has been asking everyone who's come in to pray for Gram."

"Well, the Lord has answered those prayers."

"He certainly has, Ben," Laci's mom said.

Annie, one of the waitresses, came to take their orders. Dee must have asked Charlie, her cook, to put a rush on it because it seemed no time until Annie returned with chicken fried steaks for Laci's dad and brother and big baskets of cheeseburgers and fries for her and her mom.

By the time they finished eating, Laci could tell her mother was exhausted. "Have you had any sleep lately, Mom?"

"No," her dad answered before her mother had a chance to. "She's worn-out. But we didn't want to leave the hospital."

"Well, why don't we go check on Gram again, and then you and Mom can go get some rest. I'll stay at the hospital," John offered.

"No," Laci said, shaking her head, "I'll stay."

"Laci, you've been on the road all day. I know you're tired. Mom and Dad sent me home last night. I can stay. All I have to do is call a nurse if Gram needs anything."

"Well, let's go check on her, and then we can decide what to do," Laci's mother said, grabbing her purse.

Laci could tell she was anxious to get back to the hospital and see for herself how Gram was doing. They waved at Dee while her dad and John went to pay.

When they got back to the hospital, they found Gram looking quite perky. Laci had an idea it was because of the visitor sitting in the chair beside the bed.

William Oliver stood when they entered the room and grinned at them. "Isn't it wonderful to see Ellie on the road to recovery?"

"It certainly is, Will," Laci's mother said as she patted him on the back. "And she's looking even better than she did when we went to grab a bite to eat."

"That's because the doctor came in a. . .few minutes ago and said. . .I might get to go home in a few days."

"Oh, Mother, that is wonderful news!" Laci's mom said, giving her a hug.

"I know. And there is no need for anyone to stay with me tonight. I'll probably sleep like a baby."

"But, Mother—"

"Lydia, dear, you need to go home and sleep in a real bed."

"I'll stay, Gram. I'd like to," Laci said.

"No, I will," John said. "You've—"

"None of you will stay," Gram said firmly. "I'll only. . .worry about you not getting enough rest, and. . .that won't be good for me."

Laci's mom raised her eyebrow but only grinned at her mother.

"Nurses will call. . .if they need to," Gram said.

"Whoa, Gram. You must be feeling a lot better to order us around like that," John teased.

"She's been pretty feisty ever since the doctor showed up." Will chuckled. "But it's wonderful to see her acting that way again."

"Well, if you all. . .don't go home and. . .let me get some rest, too. . .I might be. . .a tad grouchy tomorrow."

The nurse chose that moment to stick her head around the corner and let them know visiting hours were over. After saying their good nights to Gram, the family filed out into the hall with Will following a couple of minutes later.

In the parking lot, Will looked back. "I sure hate to leave her there, but I know the Lord has answered a whole lot of prayers today. He'll watch over her tonight."

"Yes, He will," Laci's mom answered. "I know how you feel, though."

"I know you do, Lydia. You get some rest like your mama ordered," Will said. "I'll see you all tomorrow."

As he gave a wave and headed toward his pickup, Laci's heart went out to him. It was obvious he cared about her grandmother as much as they all did. She was glad he was in Gram's life.

❧

Eric had missed connecting with any of the Brelands or Tanners all day. As he and Sam headed into Dee's for supper, he hoped she had some good news about Ellie Breland.

The diner wasn't too busy. It was a little later than usual for their supper, but he and Sam had been to a T-ball league meeting. Sam had wanted to play for over a year, and Eric had agreed to coach this year. Sam wanted to play so badly, and none of the other parents volunteered so Eric found himself raising his hand.

Now, as they took their favorite booth at the diner, Sam was very excited.

"Hey, guys," Dee said as she approached their table. "You're kind of late tonight. I bet you're hungry, huh, Sam?"

"I'm starvin', Miss Dee. Dad's meeting went on a long time." He spread his hands apart as far as he could.

"It did?"

"Uh-huh." Sam nodded. "Dad is going to be my T-ball coach!"

"He is?" Dee looked at Eric and grinned. "Do you know what you've gotten yourself into?"

"No, but I have a feeling I'm going to find out real soon."

Dee laughed. "Yes, I'm sure you will. What will you have tonight?"

Eric had to smile as Sam opened his menu and looked it over even though he couldn't read it yet.

"I'll have a grilled cheese and french fries, please," Sam said.

"Toasted just right. Do you want milk, too?" Dee asked.

"Yes, ma'am." Sam closed his menu and handed it to Dee.

"Thank you, sir."

"You're welcome," Sam said, grinning at Eric.

Eric's heart swelled with pride in his son's manners. Joni would be so proud of him.

"And you, Eric?" Dee turned to him.

"I'll have a patty melt and fries, please. And I'd like iced tea to drink."

"Coming right up," Dee said as she took his menu.

"Oh, Dee?"

She turned back. "Yes?"

"Have you heard how Miss Ellie is doing? I haven't been able to contact Jake or Luke."

Her smile was immediate. "Yes, I have. The family was in here earlier. Ellie has been moved to a private room, and they think she'll have a complete recovery."

"Oh, that is good news."

"Yes." Dee nodded and smiled. "It's the best kind of news."

Eric let out a breath of relief for his friends. He knew they were all rejoicing tonight. "Thank You, Lord," he whispered.

"What are you thanking God for, Dad?" Sam asked.

"That Jake and Luke's grandmother is going to be all right. She had a stroke."

"She did?" Sam's brow wrinkled. "What's a stroke?"

"It's when the blood supply to the brain is disturbed in some way," Eric answered, knowing it would be hard for Sam to comprehend what it was.

"Oh." Sam nodded as if he understood what his dad was saying. "Like it doesn't go where it's supposed to?"

"Something like that."

"But she'll be all right now?"

"Yes, it sounds as though she will be."

Sam smiled. "I'm glad she's going to be okay."

Eric reached over and squeezed his son's arm. "I know you are, son. So am I."

Dee brought their supper, and when she'd left the table Eric quietly said, "Let's pray."

Sam bowed his head, and Eric did the same. "Dear Lord, we thank You that Ellie Breland is recovering from her stroke, and we ask that she continues to do so and that she makes a full recovery. Please bless this food we are about to eat and help us to live this day to Your glory. And thank You for Sam, Lord. And we especially thank You for Your Son and our Savior, Jesus Christ. In His name we pray, amen."

"And thank You for Dad, dear God," Sam added his own words. "Amen."

three

The next few days Gram continued to recover. Her speech was gradually getting better, but she was a little unsteady on her feet and would need to walk with a cane for a while. But the doctors assured them that, with therapy, she'd be back to normal soon. Everyone was looking forward to her being able to leave the hospital.

She'd already informed them she was going to her house— not to Ben and Lydia's or Nora and Michael's, not to Jake and Sara's or Luke and Rae's. Just home to her house. So Laci and her mom met Aunt Nora, Sara, and Rae at Gram's the day before she was scheduled to come home. The plan was to clean Gram's house from top to bottom so she wouldn't be tempted to get up and do more than she needed to once she was home. Her house was always clean, but they knew she'd feel she had to be up and seeing to things if they didn't take care of them for her.

Laci, Sara, and Rae took the upstairs, stripping the beds and putting on fresh sheets, cleaning the two bathrooms, and dusting and vacuuming.

As the morning wore on, Laci listened to the women teasing each other while at the same time expressing their true concern for one another. She realized how much she'd missed by being away the last few years.

She and Sara had known each other for a long time, but now she was wife to Jake and mother to his little girl, Meggie—and they had a baby due soon. Family relations got even more complicated with Aunt Nora and Rae. As Michael's daughter *and* Luke's wife, Rae was both stepdaughter and niece-in-law to Aunt Nora. The four of them—Aunt Nora and Michael, Rae and Luke—had shared a double wedding not too long ago.

What surprised Laci the most was how much her aunt Nora seemed to have changed. She didn't even seem to be the same person.

Once they got the upstairs cleaned and sparkling, Laci, Sara, and Rae decided it was time to think about lunch. After going downstairs to find out what Laci's mom and aunt wanted to eat, they called in an order and headed out the door to pick up lunch for everyone at Dee's diner.

ૐ

Eric called Jake early that morning and made plans to meet at the diner for lunch. Jake was already there when Eric arrived. He slid into the opposite side of the booth Jake was occupying, but before they could start a conversation Dee was there to get their orders. She voiced what Eric was thinking. "I can tell Ellie is better just from the expression on your face, Jake. I'm so glad."

"Thanks, Dee. We all are. I know you've been praying, and I thank you for the prayers. We know the Lord has heard many prayers for Gram and answered them."

"She's a special lady. Everyone loves Ellie. I'll try to get over to visit her soon. What can I get for you guys?"

"I'll have the lunch special of meatloaf and iced tea to drink, please," Eric said.

"I'll have the same thing," Jake said with a short nod.

"I'm helping Charlie in the kitchen today. I'll have Annie bring your orders as soon as I can," Dee said, heading toward the kitchen.

"I'm sorry I never returned your call the other day," Jake said when Dee left. "We were so worried at first and then so relieved at how well Gram was doing that I forgot."

"Don't worry about that, Jake. I'm just glad your grandmother is doing so well. When is she going to come home?"

"The doctor said barring any changes she'll get to go home tomorrow. She won't come home with any of us, though. She wants to go to *her* house. But there are plenty of us to check on her." Jake shrugged. "We'll take turns or something."

"If I can do anything. . .well, I know you probably wouldn't want me to sit with her, but if I can run an errand, take her somewhere, you know. Whatever you need—"

"Thanks, Eric. I appreciate it, man. With Sara so far along I never know when I'm going to get a call, and Meggie can be such a handful that it's hard to figure out how best we can help Gram right now."

The bell over the door of the diner jingled, and they looked over to see Sara and Rae enter with another woman who looked very familiar to Eric. Was that Laci? His heart skipped a beat as she looked their way. It was.

Jake slid out of the booth as Sara spotted him and motioned to the others to follow her. "There's my lady now."

Rae waved at the two men but continued on to the cash register. "I'll get our orders while you two visit," she called.

Sara and Laci walked over to their table, and Eric quickly slid out of his side of the booth to greet them.

"Hi, honey," Jake said to his wife. "What are you all doing here?"

"Grabbing some lunch to take back to Gram's house. We've been doing some cleaning—"

"You aren't doing too much, are you?"

"No, I'm not. I promise." Sara smiled at her husband.

"Meggie is at Mother's Day Out at church. We'll pick her up on the way back to Gram's, and she can eat lunch with us. Then I'll put her down for a nap. I hope."

Jake laughed. "Yes, 'hope' is the word."

Eric couldn't help but feel a pang of. . .loss? He hoped it wasn't envy as he watched Jake kiss Sara on the cheek. He missed that kind of interaction. He'd loved being married. Most of the time he was so busy he didn't give it much thought. But suddenly he felt a well of emptiness.

"Eric, you remember my cousin Laci, don't you? Laci, you remember Eric? He spent a lot of time at Gram's with us." Jake pulled the pretty brunette who had come in with Sara and Rae forward.

Was Jake crazy? How could he forget Laci? "Yes, of course I remember Laci."

And he did. In fact he'd always thought Laci was very cute and would like to have asked her out back in high school. But he'd always felt like she was somehow out of his league. She ran around with some of the wealthier kids in town, and he spent all his free hours working. Come to think of it, not much had changed—except he worked a lot more hours now, and his free time was spent with his son.

"Hi, Eric." She smiled at him.

The very fact that Laci remembered him somehow had Eric's heart hammering in his chest. She was even prettier than he remembered with her long brown hair curling softly around her face and her greenish-brown eyes that seemed to sparkle.

"It's good to see you again, Laci. I'm sure your family is glad to have you home, too."

"Oh, yeah, we are," Jake said.

"I'm glad to be here, too. I'm hoping I can help out."

Rae walked up then with two sacks of food. "Hi. I hate to

break up this party, but we'd better hurry if we're going to eat this warm. We still need to pick up Meggie."

"Yes, we'd better go," Sara said. "I'll see you later, dear." She gave Jake a kiss on the cheek. "It's always good to see you, Eric. Don't be such a stranger, you hear? Drop by anytime."

"Thanks, Sara."

Laci just gave a smile and a little wave before she followed the other two women out the door.

&

As the three women headed for the car, Laci hoped Sara and Rae couldn't tell how flustered she'd been at seeing Eric Mitchell again. She was thankful they were talking about picking up Meggie and getting back to the house to eat, so she didn't think they knew. But Laci's pulse was still racing, and she was glad she wasn't the one driving as she sat down in the backseat of Sara's car.

Did she remember Eric? Oh, yes. She'd never forgotten him. She'd had a huge crush on him when they were in school. He was a few years older than she was, but she'd had a couple of elective classes with him and spent a lot of her high school years daydreaming about him. He looked the same, only better. His hair was still almost black and his eyes a dark chocolate color that made her think of warm homemade fudge. A few lines around the corners of his eyes only served to make him seem even more mature and attractive.

They stopped at the church Laci had gone to all her life so Sara could pick up Meggie. It was larger now. They'd added on to it in the last few years, and now it housed a nice preschool. Laci found herself looking forward to attending services while she was here.

When Sara came out of the building with Meggie, Laci was surprised at how she'd grown. She'd been a baby the last time she'd seen her. But now she was even talking—Laci chuckled as she watched Meggie's little mouth move nonstop, no doubt telling her mother all about her morning.

Rae seemed to know what she was tickled about and joined in the laughter as they watched mom and daughter make their way back to the car. "She's a talker, that one. But, oh, how she entertains us all!"

Laci didn't think Meggie could remember her, but she seemed quite happy to meet more family as Sara buckled her into her car seat beside Laci and introduced them. "Meggie, this is Cousin Laci. She's come for a visit."

"Hi, Meggie." Laci smiled down at the child. "You've grown since I saw you last."

Sara took her seat in the front, and Rae started the car while the conversation in the backseat continued.

"I'm a big girl now," Meggie said.

"Yes, you are." She seemed even smarter than she was big.

Meggie leaned her head to the side and looked at Laci. "You're very pwetty."

"Why, thank you, Meggie. So are you." She was adorable with her blue eyes and black hair just like her daddy's. She even had Jake's dimples.

"Thank you," Meggie said. "My daddy thinks so, too."

From there Meggie seemed to remember she hadn't said hi to Rae, so she greeted her and then told them about her morning until they arrived at Gram's.

They entered the kitchen to find Laci's mother and Aunt Nora still working.

"Mother can be so stubborn at times," Laci's mom was saying as they walked into the room. She was scrubbing the sink as hard as she could. "But much as I wish she'd come stay with one of us, I know she'll only feel comfortable here."

"We can all take turns staying with her." Aunt Nora took the vegetable bin out of the refrigerator and dumped its contents into a large garbage bag.

Laci couldn't believe her aunt had made the suggestion. She had never been one to put others first—at least not when Laci lived in Sweet Springs. But she'd been hearing about how much her aunt had changed. It appeared she really had.

"Aunt Nora, there's no need for that right now. I've told Mom I can stay with Gram at least for a little while."

"Oh! We didn't hear you come back in," her mother said, turning to greet the new addition to their group. "Hi, Meggie! How was your day?"

"Come on. Let's eat, and we can discuss what we're going to do about Gram over lunch," Rae suggested, setting down the sacks she'd brought in.

"Good. Hi, Nana!" Meggie greeted Aunt Nora.

Her aunt left what she was doing and came to help settle Meggie at the table. "Hi, my dearest." She dropped a kiss on the child's head. "I love you."

"I love you, too."

Sara grabbed some paper plates out of the pantry, and they found the items they'd ordered then sat down at the table.

After Laci's mother said the blessing, it was a few minutes before anyone spoke as they fed the hunger they'd worked up that morning.

"I'll move my things over tonight or first thing in the morning," Laci said, bringing up the topic of Gram again. "You all don't need to worry about taking turns staying with Gram, at least for a few weeks."

"Can you take off from work that long?" Aunt Nora wiped the corner of her mouth with a napkin.

In no hurry to return to Dallas, Laci nodded and swallowed

the bite of the club sandwich she'd ordered. "I have a very good assistant manager, and I know I can trust her to take care of things for me for a while. If I need to, I can always go back for a few days, but right now I don't think it will be a problem. Besides, you all are married and have others to think about and take care of. Right now I can do this, so please let me."

"It does sound like the answer for now," Sara said. "I have to admit I'm not quite as energetic as I'd like to be these days, so I thank you for your offer, Laci. I just wish Gram and my grandpa were married. Then he'd be here, where he wants to be, and we wouldn't be quite so worried about her."

"I wish the same thing. They aren't getting any younger, and if this doesn't serve as a call to get those two married, there's no hope." Aunt Nora took a bite out of her sandwich.

"Well, we can all pray they decide to do it," Laci's mother said. "They love each other. That's been apparent for quite a while now."

"And I hate to see them apart when they would be so much happier together," Sara added.

"Do you think they are worried you two wouldn't want them to marry others?" Aunt Nora asked, looking first at Laci's mom and then at Sara.

"Oh, surely not." Laci's mother held her hamburger midway from the table to her mouth. "I'd love to see Mom and Will together."

"So would I," Sara said.

"Hmm. Maybe you'd better be sure they both know that," Aunt Nora said.

"Well, maybe we'd better," her mom said. She bit into her burger and chewed quietly.

By late afternoon Laci was left by herself. Her mother and her aunt had gone to see Gram. Rae had gone to meet Luke for supper, and then they were going to the hospital before heading out to the ranch. Sara and Meggie were going home. Aunt Nora had promised that she and Michael would come and stay with Meggie that evening so Sara could visit with Gram. Laci would go up after she unpacked her things at Gram's house. She did make time to call Myra and check in with her, letting her know how Gram was and that she would be staying for a while.

"Don't worry about Little Touches, Laci. I'll take care of your business for you. You use all the time you need."

"Thank you, Myra. I can't tell you how much it means to know you are handling everything there."

They talked for a while longer, and when Laci got off the phone she felt much better knowing she could trust Myra to handle the business in her absence. There were no problems that needed her attention, and she didn't have to feel guilty about not returning to Dallas right away.

But as she settled herself into the room that had been her mother's at one time, the quiet took hold, and Laci couldn't keep thoughts of Eric Mitchell out of her mind any longer. She'd been surprised to find she was still attracted to him after all these years. It was almost as if time had stood still and she felt exactly the same way she had the last time she'd talked to him.

It had been at a football game, and he'd been with Jake and Luke. All she really remembered was that her cousins had teased her about something, as they were prone to do back then, and Eric had come to her defense.

And the memory of him doing so had stayed with her all these years. She didn't know what he'd said or why, but she remembered feeling special, and from that day on he'd become her hero. She wondered about him now, then told herself it was only because she had no one special in her life right now while everyone else—except her brother—seemed to have someone. Did Eric? She didn't know.

She went to look out onto the backyard where she'd spent many days playing. Suddenly she wished she were a child again. Things were much simpler then. Now she was longing for home when she didn't even know what she was going to do about her business. Her life, such as it was, was in Dallas, but she wanted to be here.

And she was longing for more. . .so much more. The last thing she needed was to be weaving dreams about a high-school crush when her life was so mixed up.

❧

Eric forced thoughts of Laci Tanner to the back of his mind as he picked up Sam and took him to T-ball practice. He spent the next hour or so trying to concentrate on teaching little boys how to stand at home base, the right way to hold a bat and try to hit the ball off the tee, and how to catch and pitch a ball. He couldn't help but be proud of Sam and sorry for some of the boys on the team. At least Sam knew the basics. Some of these little boys didn't have a clue about what they were doing, and he wasn't sure they were there because they wanted to be or because their parents wanted them to be. He figured he'd find out in the coming weeks.

Sam was wound up the rest of the evening, and it wasn't until after Eric had tucked him into bed, listened to his prayers, and turned out the light—leaving only the soft glow from his nightlight on—that thoughts of Laci began to sneak back in. Eric straightened up the kitchen and let his mind wander back over the day. He was thankful Ellie Breland was going to be all right. He knew what it was like to lose those you loved, and Luke and Jake had lost their parents at an early age. Their grandmother and grandfather Breland had raised them.

He was glad Luke and Jake had Rae and Sara in their lives, but he had to admit that sometimes seeing them together made him long for someone special in his life. As busy as he was, though, with work and Sam and trying to keep up with everything at home, being lonely wasn't likely to change anytime soon. But. . .after seeing Laci again, he sure wished it would.

four

Gram was released the next afternoon, and the whole family gathered at her house that evening. Things seemed more normal with her at home, even though the doctor had ordered her to take it easy until he told her differently. Everyone seemed relieved just to have her out of the hospital.

Gram had more news for them. As soon as the whole family was there, she announced that Will had proposed once again that very day, and she'd *finally* accepted. But she'd made him wait to put the engagement ring on her finger until they were all together.

As Will sat down on the sofa beside Gram and slid the diamond on her ring finger, Laci felt tears of happiness well up for the two of them. She'd never been prouder of her family than at that moment—for the way they were all truly thrilled for the couple. She'd been a little concerned about her mother; but after witnessing the touching hug she gave Will and the way he hugged her back, Laci knew everything was all right.

"Well, I have to tell you we've all been praying for this," Aunt Nora said, wiping a tear from her eye. "But what made you finally decide to say yes?"

"My stroke made me realize I don't have. . .forever. We've—"

Will cleared his throat.

"*I've* wasted. . .enough time," Gram corrected, her speech still slow. "And I'm not going to waste. . .anymore. Well, only the time it takes to get my health. . .back to normal and plan the wedding. I'd really. . .like a nice one after witnessing Jake's and Luke's and Nora's. And I want *all* my loved ones. . .to be there."

Laci grinned when her grandmother looked pointedly at her. "There is no way I'd miss your wedding, Gram. I'll even help plan it if you'd like. Do you two have a date in mind?"

"Ellie thinks we ought to wait until after the election so Lydia and Ben can help John. She'd like us to do a little campaigning for him, too," Will answered.

"Gram, you don't need to put it off that long," John said.

"It takes time to plan a wedding. I. . .want a nice one. And I sure don't want to use this cane. . .to get me down the aisle. We'll see how it goes."

"Okay, but don't worry about my campaign."

"I want Lydia and Ben to help you out. I'll be fine."

"Of course you will," Laci said. "I'm going to see that you are. I'm staying to make sure you take it easy and get better. Besides, I want to help plan this wedding."

"Can you stay that long?" John asked.

"I hope so. I have a great assistant back in Dallas. If something comes up I have to take care of, I could drive back for a few days." Laci didn't tell them she was thinking of moving back to Sweet Springs.

Her mother shook her head. "Well, I don't know—"

"Mom, I can do this. It's time I helped this family some. You and Dad go help John win his election, and I'll move in with Gram for now. It's settled."

&

The next week was a busy but rewarding one for Laci. She felt good about staying with Gram and helping her. She wasn't happy about not being able to do things as normal, and Laci had to watch her constantly to make sure she didn't overdo it;

but it was wonderful to spend time with her.

Keeping up the house was not a problem. After the cleaning they'd all done before bringing Gram home, Laci took to cleaning a couple of rooms a day and managed to keep the house looking wonderful with relative ease.

She enjoyed doing the cooking—and Gram seemed to enjoy supervising. Laci loved getting Gram's secrets to making pie dough and battering chicken fried steak. Laci felt particularly proud when Gram pronounced Laci's biscuits every bit as good as her own. Laci planned on learning to make some of her favorite dishes from her grandmother's recipe file over the next few weeks.

After a few days Laci's mother seemed to relax and even acknowledged that Laci was perfectly capable of caring for Gram while she was gone.

"At least it will be easy to keep in contact. You'll have all our cell phone numbers, and I'll check in every day," Laci's mom said.

"Lydia, I'm going to be fine," Gram said. "You need to stop worrying about me. . .and do what you can to get that grandson of mine elected. Will and Laci are going to make sure. . .I follow the doctor's orders. You can be certain of that."

Laci's mother nodded her head. "I know they will. I just hate to leave you, Mom."

Laci could tell her mother was near tears and feeling torn. It was obvious she wanted to be in two places at once—here with Gram and out on the campaign trail helping her son. But Gram understood that, too.

"Honey, it's not my time to go," she assured her daughter. "If it were, I'd already be gone."

"I know." Laci's mom sniffed and nodded.

"Well, then. He'll call me home when He calls me home.

Until then we're going to live these lives. . .He's given us the way He wants us to. I'm sure the Lord wants John in the Senate. I have plenty of people here. . .to help me. John needs you and Ben."

Laci's mother took a deep breath then released it. "You're right. But I want to know all the details of the wedding plans. And it's not as if we're not going to be around. We'll be in and out of town on a regular basis."

"That's right."

"I just don't want to miss out on the fun of planning your wedding."

"We'll make sure we consult with you before making any decisions, won't we, Gram?" Laci assured her mother.

"Of course we will."

"Promise?" Laci's mom grinned at her mother.

"I promise," Gram said.

"Okay, I feel better now."

"Good. It's settled. Let's have a cup of coffee and some. . .of that vanilla wafer cake Laci made this morning. I think it may be. . .even better than mine."

&

That Sunday Gram felt well enough to attend church, and Will picked up her and Laci and drove them. Laci's heart swelled with love for the congregation she had grown up in. The members showed her grandmother how much she meant to them by coming up to talk to her, hug her, and tell her they would continue to pray for her until she was back to normal. They also welcomed Laci with open arms and offered to help out with Gram in any way they could.

They made their way up the aisle and joined the rest of the family, which was now so large they filled two whole pews. As Laci scooted in to sit beside her brother, John, she was humbled by how faithful her family had always been through the years.

But her heart ached at the realization that she hadn't been attending church in Dallas regularly the way she should have been. And she hadn't become involved in the congregation there either. Laci sent up a silent addition to the prayer being said, asking the Lord for His forgiveness and for His help to be the Christian she used to be—whether she stayed in Dallas or moved back home.

Her heart soared as she sang familiar hymns, and she let the joy of worshipping together as a family flow over her. As the minister, David Morgan, began his lesson, Laci put all else out of her mind and listened. It felt wonderful to be back in the church, and she'd never felt more at home than she did at that moment.

❧

The next week Laci and Will took turns driving Gram to her speech and physical therapists over in Roswell. Will could and would have taken her to every appointment, but he seemed to sense that Laci needed time with her grandmother. He really was a very sweet man, and Laci was happy he was going to be her new grandpa once he and Gram got married.

On the days Laci drove Gram to Roswell, they had lunch if her grandmother wasn't too tired. She wasn't up to doing a lot of wedding planning yet, but they bought bridal magazines and pored over them at home.

"I'm not ready to buy a dress. But I want to get an idea of what's in style for a woman my age," Gram said as she sat at the kitchen table and turned the pages of the magazine they'd just purchased.

"That's all right, Gram. There's no hurry yet." Laci put on hot water for the tea her grandmother loved. "And I don't want you getting too tired. We want your health back first. Then we'll find a dress that's right for you."

"I don't want anything too frilly," Gram said. "I just want something simple and pretty. It's not like it's my first wedding, when your grandpa and I eloped. That's why I'd like to have a real wedding this time."

"I think you should."

"You don't think I'm being silly?"

"No, ma'am, I don't think you are silly at all. Besides, the whole family has been waiting for you two to get married. They'd feel cheated if you and Will eloped."

"That's what Will said when I asked him. I think he's looking forward to seeing me walk down the aisle."

"I'm sure he is. I know we all are."

"I should have told him yes a long time ago." She sighed. "I don't know why I didn't."

"Well, it's a big step, Gram."

Gram chuckled. "You know, we should be having this conversation in reverse."

"What do you mean?"

"I should be reassuring *you* about all these things. You're the one who should be getting married."

"That's kind of hard to do when no one has asked me, Gram."

"You aren't dating anyone in Dallas?"

Laci shook her head. "No. Not really. I have some friends I go out with from time to time, but no boyfriend." And the only man she'd seen lately that she could be attracted to wasn't in Dallas. He was right here in Sweet Springs.

"Why don't you just move home, Laci? We sure do miss you here."

The teakettle began to whistle, and Laci made them both a

cup of tea. She'd always found it easy to talk to her grandmother. "I've been giving that some thought. But I don't want to get Mom and Dad's hopes up until I'm sure, so I haven't said anything to them about it."

"Oh, honey, they'd be so happy if you came back. We all would."

Laci took a sip of tea then sighed. "Being on my own in Dallas hasn't quite been what I thought it would be, Gram."

"I'm sorry to hear you've been disappointed, dear. But I sure hope you decide to come back here to live. Don't worry, though. I won't say anything to your parents until you make up your mind."

"Thank you, Gram. I know you won't. If it weren't for my business, it would be an easy decision. I don't know if I should sell out or open up a shop here or what. I'm very confused."

"Why don't you promote your assistant manager to manager to run your business from Dallas and open a shop here, too?"

"Well, I'm not sure I can afford to do both."

Gram nodded. "I understand. Maybe you could sell your inventory in the business to her. . .you know, the furnishings you've bought for the shop and the specialty items you carry and let her take over your clientele. She could change the name, and you could use that money to reopen your Little Touches here. I'm sure you would have lots of business here in Sweet Springs. There aren't many interior decorating shops around the area."

Laci felt hope grow. Relocating back here was what she wanted to do, but was it the right decision? She didn't know. "It sounds wonderful, but I'm not sure it's what I should do. I'll have to give it a lot of thought."

"And you need to. It's not something that should be decided overnight. And, Laci?"

"Yes, Gram?"

"Why don't you pray for the Lord's guidance and let *Him* show you what you should do?" Gram took a sip from her cup of tea as she waited for Laci's answer.

Suddenly Laci knew she'd been trying to make decisions without taking them to the Lord. If she'd done that before she moved to Dallas, perhaps she wouldn't be so confused now. "Thank you, Gram. You always give me the best advice. I'll do just that."

When Will came by a short time later, Laci decided to give the newly engaged couple some time to themselves. She headed downtown to her brother and cousin's law practice—or rather to the building next door to their offices, where John had set up his campaign headquarters. Her parents and John were leaving the next day, and she wanted to tell her brother good-bye.

With John running for office, her cousin Jake was taking care of most of the business at their law practice, but John liked to keep up with things when he was in town. Renting the building next door made it fairly easy to do that. Right now his campaign headquarters was filled with posters, flyers, and yard signs—and quite a few volunteers stuffing envelopes and manning phone lines. Laci was impressed.

John waved at her from across the room as he talked on the telephone. When he ended the conversation he hurried over to her and gave her a hug. "Hey, sis! I was just about to take a break. Want to go over to the diner and have some dessert and coffee with me?"

"Sure, if you have time."

"I'll make the time," he said, leading the way back outside and down the street.

"Wow! I guess I didn't realize how much was involved in

running for office, John."

John laughed. "Neither did I. But I love it. I love getting out and meeting with people, finding out what they'd like from their senators and representatives. Sometimes it's a real eye-opener."

"Is there anything I can do while you're out of town?"

"Sis, you're doing plenty watching over Gram so that Mom and Dad can help me out. That means more than I can tell you."

He opened the door to the diner, and Laci had to smile as the bell jingled. Dee greeted them when they walked in and immediately came to take their order. "I didn't expect to see you again for a while, John. You're leaving tomorrow, right?"

"Bright and early. But Laci came by, and I decided to take a break. I'll have a piece of your chocolate pie and coffee, please."

"I'd like the same thing, Dee."

"Be right out with it," Dee said.

Nothing in the conversation said Dee and John were anything except friends. But something about the way she'd looked at him when she asked when he was leaving and the way John watched *her* as she left the table had Laci wondering about the two of them. There seemed to be more to it.

The bell over the doorway jingled again, and Laci turned to see Eric Mitchell walk in. He glanced around to find a table and smiled when he saw her and John.

"Hey, Eric! Come and join us," John said.

With each step the man took crossing the floor, Laci's heartbeat sped up a notch.

"Hi, John, Laci." He took a seat at the table. "What are you two up to? And how is your grandmother doing?"

"Well, Laci can answer that best because she's taking care

of Gram so our parents can help me campaign."

Laci smiled. "She's doing great. When I left the house, she and Will were looking at wedding magazines."

"Who's getting married?" Eric asked.

"Gram and Will Oliver," John said.

"Are they really?" Eric looked at Laci for confirmation.

She nodded. "Yes, they really are."

"Well, I think that is fantastic!"

"What is fantastic?" Dee asked as she brought out the pie and coffee.

"That Gram and Will are finally getting married."

Dee plopped down in the empty chair at the table. "Finally?"

"Finally," John answered.

A huge grin spread across Dee's face. "I can't think of two people better suited to each other. They've been sweet on each other for a long time now. I am so happy for them. When is the wedding going to be?"

"Maybe after the election—we aren't real sure just yet. Gram wants to regain her health, and she doesn't want to have to use a cane to get down the aisle," Laci said. "I'm going to help her with the planning."

"Well, if you need anything, just let me know. Not that I know much about planning weddings, but I'll be glad to help out." Dee stood and looked down at Eric as if she just realized he was there. "I'm sorry, Eric. What can I get for you? Are you up for some pie and coffee, too?"

"Sounds good. I'll have the same thing they ordered. I skipped lunch today, and that chocolate pie looks mighty good to me."

While they enjoyed Dee's Mile-High Chocolate Pie, Laci listened to Eric and John talk about politics. But she found it hard to concentrate with her pulse racing at top speed. She hadn't expected to run into Eric, and she suddenly felt like a tongue-tied teenager all over again. She didn't know whether she was relieved or disappointed when he looked at his watch and suddenly jumped up.

"Oops! I'm running late. I have to go." He pulled some bills out of his pocket and laid them on the table. "John, have a safe trip. I don't have a doubt in my mind about the outcome of the election. You're going to be our new senator come November."

He turned to smile at Laci, and her breath caught in her throat. He had the most contagious smile.

"If you need help with your grandmother, Laci, just let me know. I'll help in any way I can."

"Thank you" was all Laci could muster as he waved and left the diner.

"Eric meant what he said, Laci," John said. "If you need anything while we're gone, he'll be glad to help."

"It was nice of him to offer, and I'll keep it in mind." She wished she would have reason to call on him, but she was pretty sure that wasn't going to happen. "Between Will and me and the rest of the family, I don't think there will be a problem. And don't look so concerned. We'll be fine. You just try to keep Mom from worrying, okay?"

"Will do, sis. Thank you for coming home. It means a lot to us all."

It couldn't mean more to anyone than it did to her. Home. There was no place like Sweet Springs.

❧

Eric hated to leave the diner—and Laci's company—but he was almost late in picking up Sam from his afternoon sitter and getting him to T-ball practice. Sam wouldn't have liked that at all. And neither would the parents of the rest of the team.

Their first game was in a few days, and Eric had already run into several parents who wanted to coach from the sidelines. No one wanted his job, but he had a feeling they'd love to tell him how to do it.

Sam and the other little boys on his team seemed to improve with each practice, and Eric didn't know who was looking forward to the first game the most—he or his son. The only thing that seemed to be missing was someone to cheer Sam on from the bleachers like the other boys had. He had no mother, no family nearby except for Eric. A vision of Laci and a big family came to Eric's mind, and he could picture them in the stands rooting for Sam.

He shook his head. He needed to quit thinking along those lines. Attracted as he was to Laci Tanner, she was no more attainable now than she had been in the past. He'd do well to set his sights on someone closer to home. Only trouble was, no one around here set his heartbeat hammering in his chest and his pulse racing double-time as the sight of Laci Tanner did. He sure wished she lived here. But her home was in Dallas, and he needed to remember that. Still, that vision of her cheering for his son wasn't an easy one to dismiss.

five

During the next few days Laci checked in with Myra to see how she was doing at the shop. Everything was going well, if a bit slow.

Myra again told her not to worry about how long she took. "It's not as though I work nonstop, Laci. I don't work on Saturdays unless by appointment, and we've always been closed on Sundays. If I have to work a Saturday, I'll take a little time off during the week. It's working out fine."

"I can't thank you enough for being such a loyal employee, Myra. If you need help, let me know, and we'll see what we can do about hiring someone part-time."

"Okay. But I don't think it will be necessary. I'm just glad your grandmother is all right, Laci. Don't worry about a thing here. Really."

When the call ended, Laci offered a prayer of thanksgiving that the Lord had led Myra to apply for the position of her assistant. She was a good Christian woman and had been wonderful to work with.

Laci was able to keep track of things through her laptop, and with online banking she could take care of the payroll and paying bills from Sweet Springs. While business wasn't booming, they were faring a little better than just breaking even. Myra was doing an excellent job while she was gone.

If she should decide to sell out and Myra wanted the inventory, Laci would be sure to make her a good deal. Or if she decided to open another shop here and keep the one in

Dallas, she hoped Myra would stay on as manager of that shop. In the meantime it wouldn't hurt to look around and see if she could find a nice, small, older home in which to set up business in Sweet Springs. Just in case.

Will had taken Gram into Roswell for her therapy that day, and Laci was meeting her aunt Nora, Rae, and Sara for lunch. She decided to walk down to the diner instead of driving. It wasn't all that far from Gram's, and she'd be able to see if anything was for sale near the small business district of Sweet Springs. She'd noticed several businesses in older homes off Main Street, so evidently that part of town had been rezoned.

As she strolled down the familiar streets, she was struck by a sudden wave of nostalgia. Sweet Springs had been a great place to grow up in, and it would be a wonderful place to—

Before she could finish the thought, Laci saw a FOR SALE sign. She caught her breath as she drew closer. There, right in front of her, was a cottage that would be perfect for a shop. It had probably been built sometime in the late 1800s or early 1900s and was charming, with a front porch that wrapped around two sides of the house. The front windows were large and would make wonderful display windows. She jotted down the phone number of the Realtor on the sign, making a mental note to check on it when she got back from town.

When she arrived at the diner, Rae, Sara, and Meggie were already there, and Laci hurried over to join them. "Have you been here long? I probably should have driven, but I walked over from Gram's."

"No problem," Sara said. "We've only been here a few minutes. The doctor was running late for my appointment, so Rae brought Meggie in to meet us."

Meggie was busy with a color sheet that Dee gave her little customers. Laci bent over and planted a kiss on top of the little girl's head. "Hi, Meggie! How are you today?"

"I'm good, Laci. Wae kept me while Mommy went to doctow." She smiled up at Laci. "How awe you?"

"I'm doing good, too."

"I'm glad. I'm hungwy, too."

"Nana Nora will be here soon, and then we'll order," Sara told her daughter.

" 'Kay." Meggie went back to coloring.

"I can't believe it's Aunt Nora who'll be the last to get here," Laci said. "She's usually the one waiting for everyone else."

"She should be here any minute now. She said she'd be a bit late. She was going to run by the hospital to drop off lunch for Dad," Rae said.

Sara chuckled. "She'll be here, Laci, but I'm sure the change in Nora has been amazing to you."

"Well, yes, it has." She smiled at Rae. "I'm assuming your dad has had a lot to do with that?"

"They are very happy together," Rae said. "It took me a while to accept the fact that he'd found someone to love after Mom died. I wasn't real happy about it at first."

"You'd have been less happy if you'd known Nora before her transformation, Rae," Sara said. "She's come a very long way."

"Well, I know Dad had a lot to do with it, but actually I think the love you and Jake and Meggie have shown Nora is what turned her around," Rae said.

Sara grinned. "Jake convinced her she would always be part of our family."

Laci knew Jake and Sara had been going together back in high school, but something happened and they broke up. Jake married someone else while Sara ended up marrying Nora's son, Wade. Then Wade had been killed in an automobile accident, and Sara lost their unborn baby in the crash and had nearly died herself. All of that happened not long after Jake's wife passed away, leaving him to raise Meggie alone. About a year later he moved back to Sweet Springs to be closer to family, and he and Sara fell in love all over again.

"I guess Aunt Nora wasn't too happy about you and Jake getting together," Laci said to Sara.

"You're right. She wasn't happy at all. But with the Lord all things are possible, and He was the one who changed Nora's heart. And what a blessing it's been to see it all happen right before our eyes."

"Well, she is a wonderful stepmother," Rae said. "She helped me when I was having a hard time accepting that she and Dad were in love and when I was so confused and afraid to let myself fall in love with Luke."

"You know, this family circle of ours could sure be confusing to people, couldn't it?" Laci said with a chuckle.

"It sure could. My grandpa is engaged to my grandmother-in-law, who has been my grandmother-in-law twice. Nora, who was my mother-in-law, is now my aunt-in-law, and, Laci, I am your cousin-in-law for the second time."

They were still laughing when Aunt Nora showed up. "What's so funny? What did I miss?"

"Oh, we were just talking about our family ties, Nora," Sara said. "They are pretty—"

"Amazing," Rae said.

"Yes, they are. And yet there hasn't been a divorce in the family!" Aunt Nora said.

"And that's a blessing," Sara said.

"It certainly is—especially in this day and time."

Aunt Nora kissed Meggie, who was giggling because her mommy and the others had been, and then took a seat. "I love this family. I know I didn't always show it, but, oh, how happy

I am that I'm still part of it!"

"We're glad, too, Aunt Nora," Laci said honestly. Her aunt had been a widow for a long time, and heartache had probably been part of the reason she'd been so bitter and selfish when Laci was growing up. Happiness had been a long time coming for her aunt Nora, even if a lot of it had been her own doing. Laci could only be happy for her now.

"Nana's heaw. Can we eat now?" Meggie asked.

"You sure can," Dee said, coming to take their order. "What would you like, Meggie?"

"A gwilled cheese, please. And fench fies."

"Grilled cheese and fries coming up. Want milk to drink?" Dee asked Meggie.

Meggie scrunched up her nose and looked at Sara. "Can I have chocolate milk, Mommy?"

"Yes, you can have chocolate milk."

Meggie smiled and showed her dimples. " 'Kay."

Laci couldn't help but chuckle. She was a delightful child.

Once Dee had their orders and left for the kitchen, Aunt Nora asked, "How are the wedding plans coming along? Do you need any help, Laci?"

"Well, Gram is looking at magazines and talking about it, but she hasn't been up to looking at dresses yet. Nothing has been decided about flowers or a cake and all that. Gram promised Mom we wouldn't make decisions without her input, too, so we're jotting down 'maybe' lists."

"We'd all be more than glad to help plan, too," Aunt Nora said.

For the first time Laci realized they probably would like to be in on it. "Why don't we get together with Gram once or twice a week to throw out ideas? I'm sure she'd love it."

"Oh, that would be fun!" Rae said. "Gram was in on the

planning of all of our weddings."

"I'd love to help, too," Sara said.

Meggie looked up from her coloring. "Me, too."

"Wouldn't it be fun to give her a surprise shower like you gave me, Nora?" Rae said.

"Oh, I *like* that idea," Aunt Nora said.

"I love it! That would be so much fun." Laci found herself wishing she'd been here for Rae's shower and for the fun of planning all their weddings, too. But she couldn't go back and undo the past. She'd just be thankful she was here to help with Gram's now.

"Let's do it!" Aunt Nora said as Dee returned with their drink orders. "Want to help us, Dee?"

"Help with what?" Dee asked, setting Meggie's chocolate milk in front of her.

"We want to give Gram a surprise wedding shower," Sara said as Dee placed iced tea in front of her, Laci, and Rae.

"Oh, that sounds like fun. I'd love to be part of it!" Dee said, putting a glass of water and a cup of coffee in front of Nora.

"Good, then we'll count on your help," Aunt Nora said.

"Please do. And I'll be right back with your meals," Dee said.

Aunt Nora said a blessing before their food came. "Dear Lord, we thank You for this day and for this family we are part of. Please help us make Ellie and Will's wedding as special as they are. Please bless this food we are about to eat. In Jesus' name we pray, amen."

"Amen," Meggie echoed.

Dee returned with their meals and set hamburger baskets in front of Rae and Laci and a grilled cheese down for Meggie. "Have you heard from your mom and dad, Laci? Will she be able to help with the planning?"

"Oh, yes. She'd never let us forget it if we left her out. But we can do the preliminary planning—she just wants to be in on the final decisions. I think they're coming home for a few days next week."

Dee set a chicken salad sandwich in front of Nora and a BLT down for Sara. "How is the campaign going? Did they say?"

"Really well. Mom says John is drawing good crowds at all the stops."

"That's great. I know he's going to win."

"We're sure of it," Aunt Nora said.

Dee smiled and nodded, but Laci thought she noticed a wistful expression in her eyes. Evidently she wasn't the only one who thought so.

Sara shook her head as Dee left the table. "I wish that brother of yours and Dee would come to their senses and admit they love each other." She sighed.

"Oh, so do I!" Laci said. "But I wasn't sure if I was imagining the way they look at each other or not."

Aunt Nora shook her head. "You aren't imagining it. Those two have been denying how they feel for years now. I don't know what it will take to get them together."

"Well—" Sara began but then stopped midsentence when the bell over the door jingled. They all looked up to see Luke, Jake, and Eric enter the diner.

"Look who's here," Rae said.

Laci's pulse quickened at the sight of Eric and began to pick up speed as the three men waved and headed in their direction.

"Daddy!" Meggie yelled out. "Want a fench fie?"

"Sure do." Jake reached down and took one off her plate. He kissed her cheek. "Thanks, darlin'. Let's drag a table over so we can all sit together."

The men made quick work of putting the tables together, and in the process of moving around so Jake could sit between Sara and Meggie and Luke beside Rae, Laci somehow ended up sitting beside Eric. Not that she was complaining, but it did nothing to slow down her racing pulse.

Annie came to take the men's orders, and before long three different conversations were going on at the table. Laci knew the Tanner-Breland women had developed a knack for keeping track of more than one conversation at a time. She was glad she could still do it after being away for so long.

"How you feeling, hon?" Jake asked Sara.

"Real good today. The doctor says all is well with the baby."

"I'm glad."

"I thought you were working at the ranch all day," Rae said to Luke.

"I'd planned to, but without you to have lunch with, it got lonesome so I decided to come find you."

"Missed me, did you?"

"No doubt about it," Luke answered his wife.

The caring conversations between the couples left Laci longing for the same kind of relationship. . .something she hadn't given much thought to in a while.

"How are you doing, Eric? I've been telling everyone about the excellent work you do since you helped us remodel the kitchen," Aunt Nora said.

"Why, thank you, Mrs. Wellington. I appreciate all the business you throw my way."

"You do remodeling, Eric?" Laci asked. The older home she wanted to look at would probably need some work to turn it into a shop.

"He does it all," Jake said. "He built our house. You need

to stop by when you have a minute and see what a great job he did."

"And he does excellent remodeling, too," Aunt Nora said. "He totally redid our kitchen, and we absolutely love it."

If Laci wasn't mistaken, Eric seemed to flush at the compliments.

"Why, thank you all. Maybe I need to put up a satisfied customer page on my Web site." Eric chuckled, and the color deepened.

Laci found his modesty about the work he did endearing.

"Anytime," Jake said. "We'll be glad to let people know what a great builder you are."

"Thank you. When I have time to update, I may take you up on the offer."

Annie brought out the men's food, and the next hour was one of the most pleasant Laci had spent in a long time. She hated for it to end, but when Meggie started yawning and Sara did the same, it seemed time to call it an afternoon.

"I guess I'd better get Meggie and myself home for a nap," Sara said with a chuckle.

"I need to be going, too. I have some errands to run," Aunt Nora said.

Annie brought their checks, but Jake grabbed them before anyone could pull out a wallet.

"My treat, ladies." He gave Annie a check card. "Put it all on there, please, Annie."

"Sure will. I'll be right back with your receipt." She walked over to the cash register.

"Why, thanks, Jake," Laci said

"Yes, thank you, dear," Aunt Nora added.

"Would you mind giving me a ride back to Gram's, Aunt Nora? I walked down, but I forgot how warm it would be by this time of the afternoon."

"I'll be glad to." Aunt Nora stood up and brushed at her skirt. She hugged Meggie. "Nana is going to come get you for a few hours tomorrow, okay?"

" 'Kay." Meggie yawned again as Jake picked her up to take her to the car.

"We'll see you all later," Rae said. She and Luke and Eric had decided to stay awhile longer.

"See you later," Laci said as she walked to the door. She glanced back to find Eric's gaze on her, and her heart did a funny little jump. When he waved and smiled, she waved back before following her aunt out the door.

Laci wondered how she could ever have thought of this town as boring. If she kept running into Eric Mitchell like this, any boredom she might have felt there at one time would certainly be a thing of the past.

six

Later that evening Laci told Gram and Will about Sara, Nora, and Rae wanting to be in on planning their wedding, and Laci could tell they were both pleased.

"Why, that's sweet of them. Sometimes I wonder if we ought to just elope—"

Will shook his head. "Now, Ellie, that'd be fine with me. But you know you don't want to do that. You've already said so."

"Gram, you'd better *not* do that. We all want to see you two walk down the aisle. And it will be fun to put it all together." Laci chuckled. "Even Meggie wants to help."

Gram's eyes lit up. "Oh, wouldn't she make a cute flower girl?"

"That's a wonderful idea, Ellie. Meggie would make an adorable flower girl!" Will agreed.

"I suggested we all get together and throw out ideas," Laci said. "We can do that much without Mom. Then when she gets into town we can have some of it narrowed down. Unless you decide definitely that you want something. I don't think Mom would put a damper on your fun."

"No, she wouldn't. I know she wants to be in on it all, too, though. It'll be fun just to start gathering ideas for her to help with when she comes home."

"Well, we can do that. I'll call and see if they can come over on Tuesday or Thursday when you don't have therapy, or we could get together on a Saturday or Sunday afternoon."

"That will work. Most Saturdays would be okay, but not

tomorrow. It's the Teddy Bear Brigade afternoon."

"Teddy Bear Brigade? What's that?"

"It's the nickname for a group of women at church who get together there once a month to stuff teddy bears. We take them to the local hospital and fire and police departments to give out to children who might need them. We used to meet on Tuesdays but found that left out the women who work outside the home, so we changed it to Saturdays. And we used to meet once a week, but now we have so much help we only need to meet once a month. We have a potluck lunch and then get to work."

"Oh, yes, I remember Mom's mentioning you all do that."

"Well, we'll be going this Saturday. When you call the girls, remind them of it, will you?"

"Of course I will, Gram. I'll go make those calls right now. I'll bring back a piece of cake and some coffee for you and Will after I'm finished calling, okay?"

"That sure sounds good to me," Will said. "Thank you, Laci."

She was coming to think of that gentle older man as her grandpa. She'd been young when her own passed away. And her dad's parents had died before she was born. It would be good to have a grandpa again.

It took several calls back and forth to settle on Tuesdays and Thursdays for their wedding-planning sessions with the others. She almost forgot to remind them about the Teddy Bear Brigade on Saturday, but they all assured her she could let Gram know they would be there.

Laci cut three pieces of butternut pound cake and filled coffee cups, loading it all on a tray to take to Gram and Will. As she left the kitchen she realized she was happier than she'd been since she'd moved to Dallas. The only thing missing was that someone special to share her life with. Thoughts of Eric's smile suddenly flashed through her mind, and she stopped short when she reached the living room. Where had they come from?

"Laci, dear, are you all right?"

She gave a little shake of her head to clear her thoughts. "I'm fine, Gram. I just talked to all the girls. They promised to meet with the Teddy Bear Brigade tomorrow."

"Oh, wonderful. It will be so good to have you all there."

Laci passed out the cake and coffee and visited with Gram and Will. But thoughts of Eric hovered in the back of her mind for the rest of the night and into her dreams.

෪

Eric pulled the sheet up over Sam's shoulders and smoothed back the hair on his son's forehead. It had taken him only a few minutes to fall asleep. He'd practiced hard tonight then played outside while Eric mowed the yard. The fresh air and activity had him almost falling asleep at the supper table, and once he'd had a shower and lain down, he was out like a light.

Wishing he could call it a day, Eric left the nightlight on in Sam's room and went to clean up the kitchen. He was tired, too, but he needed to unload the dishwasher before he could put in the dirty ones and then fold the towels out of the dryer. He told himself that if he were ever to marry again he wouldn't take his wife for granted. A woman's work was never done, and as a man trying to fill both pairs of shoes he figured her job was harder.

All that boring day-in, day-out stuff of keeping a home and making sure the clothes and sheets were clean, deciding what to make for dinner, shopping for groceries. . . Eric shook his head. He went to the store only when they had nothing left in the house to eat. Sometimes he and Sam ate out for several days before he broke down and went. Then he bought enough to last for as long as he could. The refrigerator and freezer were packed when he got home, but other than to buy milk and bread he didn't have to go as often.

He treated their clothing much the same way. Buy a lot of what they needed—maybe then he wouldn't have to wash as often. Only that didn't work so well anymore. Sam was growing too fast, and it was hard to keep up with him.

Eric turned on the dishwasher then pulled a pile of towels and washcloths out of the dryer and brought them to the kitchen table. He sighed as he began to fold the towels— something he did often in spite of having bought so many. A woman must truly love a man to be willing to take on all those chores willingly. And if a man was blessed with having a wife who loved him that much, he shouldn't take her for granted.

He began folding the washcloths, and his thoughts drifted to that afternoon. For a moment, seeing the loving relationships Jake and Luke enjoyed with their wives had dampened his spirits. He'd had that once. And he wanted it again. But, as busy as he was, it didn't seem likely. And the only woman who'd caught his interest lately would be going back to Texas one of these days. Still. . .he sure had enjoyed sitting by Laci this afternoon. He wouldn't mind getting to know her better. He wouldn't mind that at all.

 za

It was the next morning before Laci called about the house she'd looked at on Fourth Street. The price wasn't that bad, especially compared to what she was paying in rent for the shop in Dallas. But what made the possibility of moving back to Sweet Springs even more appealing was that it was for sale *or* lease. She wouldn't require a huge amount of money to get into it. But still she needed to give it more thought.

As she helped Gram settle in the car with her cane and a pile of little bears she'd made before her stroke, Laci found herself looking forward to the afternoon. Gram had suggested she make scalloped potatoes to take for lunch. Aunt Nora had said she'd be bringing fried chicken, and Sara and Rae were bringing salad and dessert.

When they arrived at church and went into the fellowship hall, Laci helped Gram find a place with some of the other ladies at one table then took their food into the kitchen. They'd enlarged it since she'd been away, and it was a good thing. The old kitchen barely had room for one or two ladies at a time. But this one was much larger and had plenty of room for the ten women working in it. They all seemed to be talking at once while setting out the meal on a table near the kitchen.

Gina Morgan, the minister's wife, was about Sara's age and seemed very nice. Laci also recognized Ida Connors and Susan Mead, who were close to her mother's age. And there were others she'd known for years; being here felt like home. She and her cousins-in-law pitched in with the setup, and soon they were ready to eat.

Gina asked a blessing for their work and the food. "Dear Lord, we ask You to bless the little children who will receive our teddy bears. We hope they give them comfort when they are hurting or sad. We ask You to bless this food we are about to eat, and, Father, we thank You for all our many blessings—especially for Your Son and our Savior, Jesus Christ. In His precious name we pray, amen."

Laci filled Gram's plate so she wouldn't have to navigate with her cane and took it to her; then she went back to fix her own. She brought it to the table and listened while conversations flowed around her.

"I sure hope you get better soon, Ellie," Ida said. "I'm missing your Sunday night suppers."

"I miss them, too, Ida. I'm hoping the doc will let me put away this cane when I go back to see him."

"I hope so, too. Your speech seems to be back to normal," Gina said from across the table.

Gram nodded. "It is—unless I try to talk too fast. Then I stumble some."

"We're all praying for you to get well soon."

"Thank you. I appreciate it and count on it more than you know. And I'll be having a Sunday night supper as soon as I can—I promise."

Laci remembered her mother had mentioned that Gram had started holding Sunday night suppers not long after she went to Dallas. After church on Sunday nights, anyone who wanted to come was invited. It sounded like a lot of fun, and Laci wondered if she could help her grandmother start them up again.

As lunch finished, the tables were cleared and teddy bears brought out to stuff. Made out of any kind of scrap of fabric, their faces were either painted on with fabric paint or embroidered by those with that talent. But either way they were sweet.

They became even cuter as they were stuffed. They had a tag sewn on that gave the name of the church, the address, and phone number and also said "Made with Love." Laci was sure they would be a comfort to any child in distress or pain.

She enjoyed being part of the group and felt as if she'd done something worthwhile when the bears were all stuffed and everyone got ready to leave.

"I'm so glad you're going to be with us for a while," Gina said. "I know your family is glad you're here. And I think you've been very good for Miss Ellie. She seems almost back to normal."

Laci looked over to where her grandmother was showing her beautiful engagement ring to several ladies her age. She did look so happy. "I think she's almost there."

"We are so glad she and Will are getting married. You're never too old to fall in love."

"I sure hope not." Laci grinned at Gina. "At least that would mean there's still hope for me."

"You're young yet, Laci. But I can tell you, it will probably happen when you least expect it."

"Well, it can happen anytime then." Laci laughed. But suddenly she knew she really, truly wished it would.

❧

Will and Gram had made plans to eat dinner in Roswell with friends, and Laci thought she would enjoy making dinner for herself. But after she had made five trips to the pantry and opened the refrigerator at least four times, she realized it wasn't that she couldn't find anything she wanted to eat—she just didn't want to spend the better part of the evening alone.

She thought about going over to Luke and Rae's or Sara and Jake's, but that didn't seem to be the answer either. Happy as she was for them, seeing them together at times made her long for something she didn't have—a loving relationship. And after her talk with Gina that afternoon, she was already feeling a little forlorn over that. So she decided to go eat at the diner. Dee was the only other woman her age who seemed to be in the same boat.

One good thing came from waiting so long to make up her mind on what to do. By the time she reached the diner, the supper crowd had thinned out some. She seated herself at the counter so she could visit with Dee if she had a lull, and ordered a patty melt and hash browns.

"Do you ever take a day off, Dee?" she asked after her order had been placed and Dee brought her iced tea to the counter.

"Sure I do. But with my apartment upstairs it's hard not to be here. Besides with Mom moved away and no family here"—Dee shrugged—"this—and church—are where I have contact with other people."

"I can understand that. I get awfully lonesome in Dallas."

"Why don't you move back here?"

Laci paused before answering. "Well, I'm not going to say I haven't thought about it a lot lately. But. . ."

"It's a big decision, I know. For what it's worth, I'd love to see you back here. If you opened a shop, I'd probably be your first customer. I've been thinking of redecorating my apartment upstairs. It could use a new look."

"I'd be glad to look at it for you, Dee. Anytime."

"Thanks, Laci. I could use the advice. But I'm trying to get you back here. So if you open a shop here, you could really help me out. And as a satisfied customer I'd tell all my customers about you."

"Now that sounds like a deal that would be hard to refuse. I could even give you a discount for that kind of word-of-mouth advertising."

"Well, think about it."

"I will." Laci nodded.

The bell over the door jingled, and Dee looked over and began to smile. "Well, look here. It's my very favorite customer. How are you, Sam?"

Laci turned around, and her breath caught in her throat. Eric Mitchell had entered the diner with a little carbon copy of himself by his side. And he was adorable as he marched across the room and climbed up on an empty counter stool beside Laci.

"Hi, Dee! We've been playin' T-ball and watchin' baseball at the park all afternoon. Our team won, and Dad said I could have a milkshake with my supper. And so that's what I want. A grilled cheese and fries and a chocolate milkshake." The little boy barely took a breath between sentences. "Didn't you say so, Dad?"

"I did. We need these to go, though, Dee. I have to get him home and calmed down, or we'll never make it to Sunday school tomorrow."

Dee nodded, acknowledging his comment while she talked to Sam. "Well, congratulations! And since you won, the shake will be on me. Think we ought to treat your dad to one, too, since he coached the team?"

"Sure! He's the best coach ever."

"Okay, what else will you have, Eric?" Dee asked.

Laci didn't hear Eric's answer. She was too busy trying to take in everything. *Dad. Eric was a dad.* Her heart sank a little further each time she thought about it. Eric Mitchell had a child. She hadn't thought Eric was married. . .but obviously he must be. Still, he didn't wear a wedding ring. Was he divorced? Either option made the dreams she'd begun to weave about Eric wither in her heart. She willed herself not to show how disappointed she was.

"Hi, Laci. How are you tonight?" Eric asked as he took a seat on the other side of Sam.

"I'm fine." She looked down at his little boy and found big black eyes looking at her. She smiled at him. "Congratulations on winning your game."

"Thank you." He kept looking at her and then asked, "Who are you?"

"Sam!"

"I'm sorry, Dad." He looked back at Laci. "Dad doesn't like me to talk to strangers," he said in explanation.

"No, I don't. But I know Miss Tanner. I was trying to get you to realize you just sounded rude."

"I'm sorry. I didn't mean to. I just don't know who she is."

Eric sighed and shook his head. "Sam, this is Laci Tanner."

"Is she relationed—I mean *related*—to Jake and Luke and Sara and Rae and Meggie?"

"She is. She is their cousin."

"Oh, hi!"

"Hi, Sam. It's nice to meet you." Laci tried hard to concentrate on the little boy and not the man beside him. She had no business thinking about Eric Mitchell.

"You're nice. Do you like T-ball?" Sam asked.

"I don't think I've ever watched T-ball."

His eyes seemed to grow larger—if that was possible. "Really? You never have?"

"No, I never have. I bet it's fun to play, though."

"Uh-huh, it is. I have a game next week if you want to watch one."

"It's on Tuesday afternoon if you'd like to come," Eric said.

Laci wasn't sure what to say, and she wasn't at all happy with Eric for putting her in the awkward position of having to disappoint his son. "I'm not sure. I may have to take Gram to Roswell for her treatment."

"If you can't make it then, there'll be another one on Saturday," Eric said.

Laci knew Will would be more than happy to take Gram to Roswell, but she had no intention of going to the game. She just didn't want to come out and say so.

But the pressure was on when Sam looked up at her and

smiled. "I'd sure like you to come see a T-ball game."

"I'll see what I can do," Laci found herself saying non-committally. "I hope you win again."

"Me, too!"

Dee came back with Eric's orders to go, and Laci felt a sense of relief that he would be leaving soon.

Eric paid Dee and turned to Sam. "Come on, son. I have to do a load of wash when we get home."

"Okay," Sam said, climbing down from the stool and following his dad to the door. But he looked back and waved. " 'Bye."

" 'Bye," Laci and Dee both said at the same time.

Sam tugged at the door to open it for his dad.

"Thank you, Sam." Eric looked back for a moment. " 'Bye, ladies. See you later."

Laci didn't realize she'd released a huge breath when they left until Dee asked, "Laci, are you all right?"

"I—I didn't know Eric had a child. I didn't think he was even married."

"He's not. His wife died when Sam was only a few months old."

"Ohh." Her first reaction was relief that she wasn't attracted to a married man, quickly followed by sadness at his loss. And then there was Sam. . .so adorable and without a mom. Just thinking about him tugged at her heart. Sudden tears formed behind her eyes. "What did she die from?"

"She had a rare form of cancer. They didn't even know about it until she got sick."

"That's awful." And it was.

"But Eric was so strong through it all. And he is such a good dad to Sam."

Laci could only nod in agreement. She was glad Dee had

to hurry off to wait on new customers who entered the diner. She didn't know what to say when her heart seemed to be sinking like a rock.

Eric was a single dad with a cute son. But that was a ready-made family and completely different from a single man who'd never been married. No matter how wonderful a dad Eric was—and Laci was sure he was a great one—his son needed a mom. And Laci wasn't sure she was nurturing enough to be the kind of mother Sam would need.

She let out another deep breath and forced herself to take a bite from a cold french fry. She needed to get Eric Mitchell out of her mind and quit weaving dreams about him. And she needed to do it now. But that was easier said than done when she remembered Sam's sweet invitation to come watch him play ball.

seven

Laci's parents came in for the weekend, and Jake and Sara invited the family over for a cookout after church on Sunday. It was the first time Laci had been in their house, and she was very impressed with Eric's talent as a builder. It was a beautiful custom home.

The home looked and felt as if it had been built around the same time as Gram's, with big bay windows and a wonderful wraparound porch. It was furnished with antiques and traditional furniture, and each room was warm and homey and welcoming. But the kitchen was Laci's favorite room. It had tiled countertops and state-of-the-art fixtures and appliances. It was laid out in an easy pattern for working, but large enough for several people to work in at the same time.

The covered patio out back was spacious and shady and a great place for family gatherings. The men stood around the grill talking while Jake cooked, and the women took charge of the kitchen to prepare the side dishes.

Sara set Laci to work grating cheese for the baked potatoes at one end of the huge island while Rae and Aunt Nora put together the salad at the other end. Laci's mom watched over her baked beans that were in the oven, and Gram sat at the table supervising it all. Meggie sat beside her, coloring and watching everything.

"Do you think those potatoes should come out and go in the warmer, Sara, dear?" Gram asked.

"I think they're fine, Gram."

"Nora, don't chop that lettuce too fine, please. It gets stuck between my teeth if it's too little."

Laci held her breath, waiting for Aunt Nora's response.

"All right, Ellie. I didn't think of that."

Laci saw her aunt wink at Rae and grin, and she felt herself relax. At one time Aunt Nora would have had a comeback for Gram, but she had definitely changed. And then again she might have let it pass back then—they all knew Gram and her heart very well—and loved her the way she was.

"I'll be glad when the doctor releases you from his care, Mom." Laci's mother grinned at Gram and teased, "You've become quite bossy since your stroke."

Meggie sidled up to Gram and patted her back. "Gwam not bossy, Aunt Lydy."

Gram chuckled and hugged the child. "Thank you, Meggie. But your aunt Lydia is right."

"You admit it, Mom?" Laci's mother smiled at Gram.

"I've always been a little on the bossy side, Lydia, and you know it."

"Oh, I guess you have, come to think of it." Laci's mom laughed. "And I wouldn't have you any other way. I'm glad you're feeling well enough to give orders from over there."

"No one is going to be happier than I will be to get back to normal. Laci is a wonderful cook, but I miss puttering in my kitchen. I miss my Sunday night suppers, too. I want to get back to those as soon as I can."

Aunt Nora said, "We could take over—"

"No. If I didn't know I'd be getting better, I'd say yes. But it's something I enjoy doing. One of these days, though, when I can't manage it, you will all need at least to take turns at it. I don't want the custom to die out."

"We won't let that happen, Gram," Rae said.

"I'd be glad to help you hold one now if you want," Laci offered.

"I'll see what the doctor says this week."

"Michael thinks you are making wonderful progress," Aunt Nora said.

"Well, I wish he was my doctor for this, but I'm glad he sees some improvement." Gram changed the subject. "How is John's campaign coming along, Lydia?"

"I think it's going very well. He had a rally in Farmington planned for today, and I'm sure it will go fine. He has great crowds showing up to hear him speak everywhere we've been. And the contributions to his campaign are flowing in."

"That's wonderful. He's going to make a great senator. I just know it," Laci said with sisterly pride.

"I do, too. And I'm sure he's going to win," her mother said. "I'd feel a little more confident, though, if he were married, as his opponents are."

The doorbell rang just then, and Sara wiped her hands on a dishcloth. "Jake invited a couple of more people today. They must be here now." She hurried to answer the door and was back within minutes with Eric and Sam following her.

"Hi, ladies," Eric said.

Everyone else greeted him while Laci's heartbeat did a little tumble of some kind. Then it began to beat so hard she was afraid they all could hear it. She certainly felt it. She barely managed a hello.

"Hi, Lace!" Sam said with a grin, pulling her attention away from his dad. "I didn't know you was going to be here today."

He was so engaging that Laci couldn't help but smile. "I didn't know you were going to be here either, Sam."

"You gonna come to my game on Tuesday?" He smiled up at her, waiting for her answer.

Laci's heart melted at the look in his eyes—and the hope-fulness in his voice. She knew she shouldn't get his hopes up, but she couldn't tell this little boy no. "I will try to be there, okay?"

"Okay, Lace!"

"It's Laci, Sam," Eric corrected.

"It is?"

"It's all right, Sam. You can call me Lace if you want to." She liked it.

"See, Dad? It's okay. Lace says it is."

Eric grinned and shook his head at his son. "All right, son. Let's go outside and see what Jake and the other men are up to, okay?"

"Sure. Let's go outside with the other men." He looked back into the room. "See ya."

There was a moment's quiet as the women in the room watched him follow his dad outside.

"Oh, wow! He is going to be a little heartbreaker one day," Rae said.

Sara chuckled. "Is he ever! I'm going to keep Meggie away from him."

"No, Mama. I like Sam. He's nice," Meggie said.

She'd been so quiet with her coloring that everyone must have forgotten she was there.

"I'm teasing, sweetheart." Sara gave her daughter a hug before turning to Laci. "So, *Lace*, how did you meet Sam?"

"Gram and Will went out last night, so I ate at Dee's. He and Eric came in, and we sort of hit it off."

"You and Eric?" Rae asked, grinning at her.

"No. Sam and I."

"Oh, I see," Laci's mom said, sounding a little disappointed.

Gram nodded. "I do, too."

Laci could feel the color rise up her neck and onto her face for no real reason except that everyone seemed to be watching her. "What?"

"Nothing, dear." Her mom patted her on the shoulder and teased, "It's just too bad Sam's not a little older. He seems quite taken with you."

"He is adorable," Sara said. "Jake suggested inviting them over today. It must get lonesome for Eric at times, especially on a Sunday."

"I imagine he's kept busy on the weekends just trying to catch up from the past week. It can't be easy for a man to try to be both mom and dad to a child," Aunt Nora said.

Laci was sure it wasn't. But it was plain he was doing a pretty good job. Sam seemed to be a wonderful child.

"A man needs a wife," Gram said.

"And speaking of that," Laci's mother said, changing the subject, "how is the wedding planning going?"

"We've decided to meet on Tuesdays and Thursdays to do the preplanning. Then when you get to come home for a few days, you can help with the final decision making," Gram said.

Laci's mom crossed the room and hugged her mother. "Thank you for finding a way to include me."

"You're welcome, dear."

Jake opened the back door just then and stuck his head inside. "Steaks are about ready. How are things in here?"

"We're ready whenever you are."

"Good. Just bring it on out anytime now."

Sara and Laci quickly filled glasses with iced tea, and everyone helped carry them outside. Then they brought out the rest of the food. After Jake said the blessing, Sara and Eric fixed their children's plates, and then the adults helped themselves.

"Come and sit by me, Lace," Sam asked when Laci turned from filling her plate. He and Meggie were sitting at the end of the line of tables Jake had set up.

"Sit by *me*, Laci," Meggie insisted.

Laci couldn't refuse either of them. So she took her tea and her plate and sat down between Sam and Meggie. They entertained her by explaining what they liked about their meal.

"I like steak. It's kind of hard to chew, though," Sam said.

"I like the potato best," Meggie said. "It's easy to chew."

"I like the salad," Laci told them.

"It gets stuck between my teeth," Sam said with a disgusted look on his face.

Laci had to chuckle. She'd have to remember to tell Gram she wasn't the only one that happened to.

Sara and Jake joined them as did Eric. Laci tried hard to keep her attention on the children, but she couldn't ignore the man sitting directly across from her as conversation flowed around the table. It was impossible not to steal a glance at him from time to time, and when she did she invariably caught his gaze on her, sending the color rushing to her face once more. She could only hope Eric thought she was sunburned.

❧

Eric found it hard to keep from staring at Laci as she gave most of her attention to his son and Meggie. She was very good with them. That Sam liked her so much told him a lot. Eric had never seen him take up with anyone quite so fast. But something about Laci drew Sam to her since they'd met the night before, and he'd talked about her the rest of the evening after they left the diner.

Not that Eric blamed him. His son had excellent taste. Eric had found himself thinking about Laci all evening, too. She'd been so sweet to Sam, and the give-and-take between the two had been fun to watch. He hoped she stayed around awhile.

The rest of the afternoon was one of the most pleasant Eric had spent in a long time. Sam and Meggie convinced Laci to play with them on the large swing set and in the playhouse Jake had put up for his daughter. At five, Sam felt much older than Meggie who was three, but Eric was pleased to see how well his son played with her.

The rest of the women were cleaning up and would bring out dessert after their meal had settled a little while. He and Jake, Luke, Michael, Laci's dad, Ben, and Will took turns playing horseshoes.

"Thanks for asking me and Sam over, Jake. We're both really enjoying the afternoon."

"I'm glad you could come over," Jake said as they watched Luke throw his horseshoe. "I couldn't help but notice you watching Laci. You interested in her?"

Eric was a little surprised by the blunt question, but he wasn't going to lie. "Well, yeah, I am, I guess. I could be even more interested if she lived here."

"That right?"

"Yes."

"Well, we're all trying to get her to move back."

Eric's heartbeat picked up at the thought that she might. "In that case I wouldn't mind if you and Sara could see your way to get us together a little more often. At least until I get a sense of whether or not she could be interested in me, and then I could ask her out on my own."

"Oh, I think we can handle that."

"Thanks, Jake. You're a good friend."

Jake looked over at where Sam and Meggie were playing with Laci and then back to Eric. "I know firsthand how badly a child needs a mom, and Laci would make a good one, even if she doesn't realize it yet."

"I guess I should go rescue her from Sam."

"I'll go, too. Meggie can be pretty persistent."

The two men walked over to the playhouse and knocked on the door.

Meggie opened it a tad. "Hi, Daddy! Did you come to play?"

"Well, not just now. We think you need to let Laci go visit with the ladies inside."

"Why? It's more fun out here. She'll have to work if she goes in," Sam said with the wisdom of a five-year-old.

Eric could hear Laci chuckle even if he couldn't see her. He peeked in a window at his son and at Laci who was sitting in a tiny chair playing as if she were enjoying pretend tea. "Sam, I think Laci might want to visit with the ladies a little while."

"Do you?" Sam looked to Laci for confirmation.

"Well, I think I ought to go help bring dessert out to you guys, don't you?" Laci said diplomatically.

"Oh, dessut!" Meggie began nodding her head. "Okay. Laci needs to go, Sam."

Sam was a little more hesitant. He sighed and leaned his head to the side. "I guess so."

"I'll go see what they have for us, okay?" Laci said as she inched her way out the door.

"Okay."

"C'mon, Sam. Let's go swing 'til dessut gets here."

The two children ran over to the swings.

"I'm sorry Sam has held you captive most of the afternoon," Eric said to Laci as the three adults started toward the house.

"Well, Meggie did her share, too. Don't blame it all on Sam," Jake said.

"They are both precious, and I've enjoyed myself," Laci

said. "I haven't been around children in a long time. You forget how refreshing their outlook on life is."

"Jake, Eric, you two part of this game or not?" Luke shouted from the side yard.

"We're coming. Let's go show them how to throw a horse-shoe, Eric," Jake said, heading across the lawn.

"Okay." Eric smiled at Laci before he turned to go back to the game. "Thanks again, Laci."

"You're welcome." Laci smiled and waved as she hurried into the house.

ત

"Thanks for entertaining Meggie and Sam, Laci," Sara said when Laci entered the kitchen.

Laci laughed. "I'm not sure who entertained whom. Those two are something." She'd enjoyed swinging and going down the slide with them and the pretend tea party. Mostly she'd just enjoyed hearing them talk. "And they are quite ready for *dessut*, as Meggie called it."

Sara laughed as she and Rae scooped out little balls of water-melon and added them to a bowl of cantaloupe balls. "It's about ready. It's not chocolate, though, so I'm not sure Meggie will consider it real dessert. They are something, aren't they? I love the way their minds work."

"Children have a way of looking at things that reminds us all of what's important," Gram said.

"That they do," Laci's mom said. "And speaking of children. . . you know your dad and I aren't getting any younger, Laci. You and John need to start thinking about settling down and starting families of your own so we can have grandchildren while we're young enough to enjoy them."

"Mom, that's not something you can just decide on. You have to meet the right person first."

"Well, how do you know you haven't?"

For some reason Laci felt that annoying blush again as her mother continued. "Actually I think John has. Only he and Dee are too blind to see it."

That led to a discussion of what to do to get the couple to admit how they felt about each other.

The back door opened, and Luke poked his head in. "Hey, we have some hungry kids out here. When is dessert coming?"

Rae grinned at her husband. "I know who the biggest kid is—you."

Luke laughed. "You know me well, sweetheart. We're working up an appetite with all this exercising we're doing."

That brought laughter from everyone in the kitchen.

"I know that pitching must be very tiring," Rae said with a grin. "We're bringing it out now."

Laci loved hearing the loving banter going on between her cousin and his wife. She could tell from the tone of their voices and the look in their eyes that they were crazy about each other. She wondered if she'd ever have that kind of relationship. She walked outside then and saw Eric's pitch make a ringer around the pole. And she wondered who it would be with if she did.

eight

Eric had known what he was missing, but he'd never felt it so acutely until now. The day had been pure joy for him and his son, and he hated to see it come to an end. So did Sam. As they said their good-byes to the Tanners and the Brelands, he felt a loss he couldn't understand.

"Thanks for having us," he said to Sara and Jake. "We enjoyed it a lot, didn't we, Sam?"

"Uh-huh! It was fun. Thank you."

"You are very welcome. I hope you'll come back again," Sara said to Sam.

"If you ask, we will," he answered matter-of-factly.

"We'll be sure to ask then," Sara assured him.

Sam turned to Laci. "Thanks for playin' with us, Lace."

"Thanks for letting me."

"You gonna come to my game on Tuesday?" he asked once more.

Laci knelt to be at eye level with him. "I'm sure going to try, okay?"

"Okay. I'll be looking for you."

When Sam suddenly threw his arms around Laci and hugged her, Eric was surprised. He'd never seen his son hug anyone but him. He saw tears gather in Laci's eyes as she hugged Sam, and he realized she'd been touched by the show of affection, too. Eric had a hard time holding back his own tears.

He turned quickly. "Let's go, pal. We need to run by the grocery store and pick up milk for tomorrow."

"Okay, Dad." Sam slipped his hand into Eric's, and they both turned and waved good-bye.

Eric nodded at Laci and mouthed, "Thank you."

She nodded, and he hoped that meant she knew how thankful he was for her attention to Sam.

If he hadn't been pretty sure Jake would keep his word and try to get them together again, Eric would have felt much worse about leaving. Something about that woman touched his heart, and it was more than how well she treated his son. She made his heart beat in a way it hadn't in years, and he liked it. He wanted to ask her out, even though the thought of dating had him feeling like a teenager all over again. Funny how some things never changed. Some feelings were the same no matter how old a person was.

"Do you think she'll come to the game, Dad?" Sam asked as he buckled up his seat belt in the backseat of Eric's pickup.

"I don't know, Sam," Eric answered honestly. "I think she will try to, though."

"I hope so."

"So do I, son. So do I." And he did—for both their sakes.

❧

Laci hadn't been prepared for the overwhelming feeling that flowed over her when Sam hugged her that afternoon. She didn't know what to call it—all she knew was that he'd claimed a piece of her heart that day. She'd planned on trying to get out of going to his T-ball game, but after that hug there was no way she could miss it.

She looked for them at church that evening but didn't see them. She tried to put Eric and his son out of her mind as she concentrated on the lesson David was bringing. It was about leaving things in the Lord's hands and turning one's worries and cares over to Him. With so many decisions she had to make, the lesson spoke to Laci. Should she sell her business? Should she move back here? Should she tamp down the growing attraction she felt for Eric? Those were questions she needed to take to the Lord in prayer. She needed His help with all of it.

Once the service was over and she and the rest of her family were heading up the aisle, she was surprised when she heard her name called.

"Lace, wait!"

She turned to find Sam running toward her with Eric following at a slower pace.

"I didn't know you came to our church," Sam said when he reached her. "Dad said you did, but I never saw you here 'til tonight."

"I sure do. Did you and your dad get to the grocery store?" She could see Eric making his way toward them.

"Uh-huh. We got milk and some new cereal to try. Oh, and bread. Dad makes pretty good grilled cheese sandwiches." He leaned closer and whispered, "Don't tell him, but Dee makes them a little better. But his are good."

"I won't say anything."

Sam grinned up at her. "Thanks, Lace. I hope you get to come to my game. Dad said you might not be able to make it, but I hope you can be there."

"I'm planning on it, Sam."

"Sam, are you pestering Laci again?" Eric asked as he reached them.

"I don't do that, do I, Lace?"

"No, you don't."

"See, Dad."

Eric sighed and grinned at Laci. "He does have a one-track mind right now. He can't think of anything but his next game.

I've told him you might not—"

"I know. But I'm going to try to come. I don't see any reason why I can't, unless something serious comes up to prevent me from getting there."

"Oh, boy," Sam said. "I'll have someone in the bleachers to root for me!"

"You don't have any relatives in the area?" Laci looked up at Eric.

He shook his head.

Suddenly Laci realized that with no mother to come to the games Sam had no one in the stands cheering for him. Her heart twisted at the thought. "I'll be there to cheer you on, Sam. I promise."

"Thank you, Laci," Eric said softly.

"I wouldn't miss it." And if she had anything to do with it she wouldn't be the only one cheering Sam on at his next game.

"Okay! See you Tuesday," Sam said before running off to join several other children.

Laci looked up to see Eric's gaze on her. "I hope he isn't bothering you. I'm at a complete loss here. Sam has never taken to anyone the way he has you."

"Well, I've never met up with anyone quite like Sam either. He's a special little boy."

Eric cleared his throat. "I certainly think so."

"Eric, please don't worry. Sam is not bothering me. I'm honored that he seems to like me." And she spoke the truth. It wasn't Sam who bothered her. It was his dad. He kept turning up in her dreams at night. . .and in the middle of the day, too.

&

On Tuesday the Wedding Planners, Inc.—as they'd decided

to name themselves—met at Gram's for lunch. Laci made salad and a pasta casserole and was just pulling it out of the oven when Sara and Rae arrived with Meggie. They'd stopped at a fast-food place and picked up chicken nuggets for her.

Aunt Nora arrived right behind them, and after Gram asked the blessing, they all helped themselves and proceeded to have a leisurely lunch.

"Are you going to Sam's game this evening?" Sara asked before taking a bite of casserole.

"Yes. I promised him I would. You know. . .he doesn't have anyone in the stands to cheer him on."

"That's right," Aunt Nora said. "Eric has no relatives here anymore. Oh, dear. Poor little thing."

"Well, I'm going. Any of you want to join me?" Laci took a sip of tea and waited for their response.

"I'll go," Gram said. "I'll get Will to go, too. What time is it?"

"It's at six thirty."

Gram nodded. "We'll go out to eat after it's over."

"Thank you, Gram. That will mean so much to Sam."

"I'll talk to Luke," Rae said. "Maybe we'll be there, too."

"I'm sure Jake would be glad to go," Sara added. "I'll check with him."

"Well, if you are all going, Michael and I will, too," Aunt Nora said. "I don't want to be left out."

"I love you all. You are the best family in the whole world," Laci said.

"Well, why don't you just move home for good then?" Sara asked.

"I'm thinking about it," Laci finally admitted. Everyone started talking at once about it, but she didn't say anymore. She wasn't quite ready to discuss her ideas.

Once they'd finished eating they cleared the dishes and

spread bridal magazines on the table. Laci's mom and dad had left on Monday to rejoin John on the campaign trail, but they were hoping to get back to town for the weekend. The girls hoped to be able to present some ideas to Laci's mom then for her input.

"Gram has marked pages in all of these. She doesn't want the normal wedding dress—"

"Just something simple and gorgeous," Gram said. "I do want to keep it simple."

"Do you have any colors in mind?"

"Not really. I'm partial to silver or cream for a wedding dress. And I'm not talking about one like you girls wore. Maybe a suit or just something kind of. . .elegant."

"Maybe you'd be happier with something that's usually for the mother of the bride," Aunt Nora suggested. "These books have those, too."

Sara flipped through one of the magazines until she came to a page with outfits like the ones Aunt Nora was talking about. "Look, Gram. Something like this?"

Gram pulled the magazine closer and nodded. "That's more like it, yes."

"Okay! I think we have an idea of what to look for now. At least style wise," Laci said. "Now you need to think about colors. Are you going to have attendants?"

"Just your mother," Gram said. "And maybe Meggie as a flower girl."

"Me?" Meggie had been coloring again, but Laci knew her well enough now to know she was listening to every word.

"Yes, you. You'll get to walk down the aisle ahead of me and throw flower petals out on the floor."

Meggie caught her breath and grinned. "I can thwow flowaw petals?"

"Yes, you can. And you'll get to wear a very pretty dress."

Rae showed her a picture from one of the magazines. "Like this."

Meggie clapped her hands. "That's pwetty! Okay."

"Where do you want the reception to be, Gram?" Sara asked.

"Oh, I think I'd like it to be in the fellowship hall at church."

Laci began to make a list of the things Gram had made a decision on and those she needed to think about. "You'll need to settle on flowers, too. What kind and color."

After about an hour they agreed to continue on Thursday. They were getting confused on what they liked and didn't like, and Gram was tired.

"I'm going to call Will about Sam's game and then take a nap. Don't let me sleep for more than an hour. Otherwise I'll never sleep tonight."

"Okay, Gram. I'll wake you," Laci said.

Aunt Nora looked at her watch. "I have to go, too. I need to check with Michael about the game and run to the grocery store. I'll see you all later."

" 'Bye, Aunt Nora. Thanks for helping."

"You're welcome. It is fun being together like this. You need to come back home for good." She gave Meggie a kiss and headed out to her car.

"You really do, you know," Sara said as she and Rae helped Laci clean up the kitchen. "We've all missed you, and it's just good to have you around."

"I'm leaning that way. I just need to be sure." And she needed to pray and hand it over to the Lord for His help in deciding. He knew what was best.

But the more she was around her family, the more she loved being with them. Just the thought of going back to Dallas left her with an empty feeling.

Eric parked the car and walked over to the ball field to practice before the game. He hoped Laci made it to the game. If not, his son would be disappointed. But he didn't want to bring up the possibility now. Besides, she'd promised Sam, and Eric thought that if something had come up she would have let him know so he could break the news to his son.

He'd watched her closely on Sunday. Laci had been touched by his son. Eric wasn't sure what she thought of *him*, but he had a feeling Sam had gotten to her. He tried to concentrate on the practice game, but he kept watching the stands as people arrived.

It was Sam who spotted Laci while Eric gathered his little guys together in the dugout just before the game started. "Dad, she's here. Lace came!"

Sure enough, Laci was there, making her way into the bleachers. She looked lovely in her green capri pants and matching top. Her hair was caught up on top of her head, and as she took a seat she waved at Sam, who had been waving his arms in the air to get her attention.

Then Sam caught his breath and let it out with a *whoosh*. "Dad!" He began pulling at Eric's shirt. "Dad—look who all she brought with her!"

It was hard for Eric to take his eyes off Laci, but it was even harder not to notice her whole family following her. Miss Ellie and Will sat on the bottom bleacher, while Sara, Jake, and Meggie took their places next to Laci on the second one. Behind them came Luke and Rae, and even Nora and Michael. Eric grinned and waved then turned away to fight the tears forming in his eyes. He blinked several times and took a deep breath. It was hard to speak around the knot in his throat, but he finally called out, "Okay, guys—batter up!"

This was the team's third game. They wouldn't start pitching until the fifth one. Sam would be the last up to bat in the first inning, and Eric hoped he wasn't the only one to hit the ball. He'd been working hard with the kids, and they'd come a long way. But they always became more nervous when their parents coached from the sidelines.

Little Eddie Morrison was up first. The umpire put the ball on the tee, and Eric made sure Eddie was in the right position to hit it. After three tries he finally hit the ball—only it landed on the ground right in front of the tee. The ball was declared dead, and Eddie tried again—and again—with his parents calling out advice from the stands.

But he kept missing. Eric wanted to tell his parents that if they'd just let him have fun he'd do a much better job, but he knew it wouldn't do any good. Eddie struck out on his last try, and it was time for the next batter in line.

Next up was Larry Dickerson. He managed to hit the ball the second time he tried, but it went straight to first base and was caught.

And on it went with cheering in the stands for each boy. By the time Sam was up they'd made one run. It seemed strange to hear all the cheers for Sam when he took his turn at bat. Eric wished he had his camera to capture the smile on his son's face when he heard Laci and the rest of her family clap and cheer as he stepped up to the tee.

The umpire placed the ball on the tee, and Eric made sure Sam was in the correct position. "Don't be nervous just because you have a fan club, okay?"

"Okay, Dad. But isn't it great?"

Eric grinned at his son. "Yes, it is. Just do your best and have fun."

Sam nodded, and Eric stepped away.

He could tell Sam was concentrating. He glanced at the stands and had the feeling that Laci and her family were holding their breath. He looked back at his son. Sam took a swing—and missed. He tried again—and missed.

As Sam got into position once more, Eric heard Laci's sweet voice call out from the stands, "It's okay, Sam. You can do it."

And do it he did. He hit the ball into the outfield and took off at a run. The other team scrambled and tried to get the ball, but they weren't fast enough. With Laci and her whole family on their feet cheering for him, Sam made a home run.

Eric knew there would be other home runs in his son's life, but he was certain Sam would remember this one for a long time. It was the first game he'd ever played with anyone in the stands to cheer him on.

The competing team was up next, and Eric sent Sam to the outfield. He knew some of the parents wanted their boys playing the bases and the infield, partly because none of them could throw very far. The only other boy on the team who could throw a ball any distance was Larry, and he played on the opposite side of the outfield. But this time they weren't needed because the other team couldn't hit a ball that far.

Still the game was tied up by the start of the second inning. Sam's nervousness seemed to have disappeared. The rotation put him batting first this time, and they scored right away, with Larry hitting another run right behind Sam.

By the end of the game Sam's team was declared the winner. They'd managed to keep the other team from getting a run when they did make a hit. They finally won by two runs, although no score was kept in T-ball.

Sam was overjoyed that Laci and her family stayed to tell him how well he played.

"Thank you!" Sam was grinning from ear to ear. "It was so

great to have someone—lots of someones—cheering for me." He looked around the circle of people congratulating him for his game. "Thank you all for coming to see me play!"

"We enjoyed it, Sam! It was fun to watch," Jake said. "You have a pretty good coach there, don't you?"

Sam grinned and nodded. "Dad's the best coach!"

"Thanks for coming, everyone. It sure meant a lot to Sam and to me, too."

"We're heading over to the Pizza Palace out on the highway for supper with Laci and Gram and Will," Jake said. "You and Sam want to join us?"

"Oh, can we, Dad?" Sam asked.

"Sure. I'd planned on stopping there anyway as a treat for Sam." He looked at Laci. "Did you drive or ride with someone?"

"I rode with Gram and Will."

Sam was a step ahead of him. "Want to ride with us, Lace?"

"We'd sure like you to," Eric added before she could answer Sam.

"Please, Lace!" Sam grinned at her.

"Yes, I'll ride with you," she said, looking at Sam.

Eric was certain it was his son who was the draw for Laci, but he wanted to get to know her better. If it took Sam to help him do that, then it was just fine by him.

nine

Jake called Eric to the side while Laci helped Sara put Meggie into their car. Gram and Will were already on their way to the pizza place. Laci wasn't sure why she'd accepted Eric and Sam's invitation to ride with them. All afternoon she'd told herself that while she wanted to support Sam she needed to be careful. She had a feeling Sam and his dad could steal her heart, and much as she wanted a family of her own she knew nothing about raising five-year-old boys.

She figured a mother learned about each age as her child grew into it—from holding him in her arms when he was born to seeing him at each stage—and that it happened over time. She told herself she was being presumptuous in even thinking about raising Sam. Eric hadn't shown that kind of interest in her. . .until now. And she was assuming a lot to think that offering to drive her to the pizza place meant he was interested in her.

Maybe it was wishful thinking on her part because try as she might she hadn't been able to keep Eric Mitchell out of her dreams. So here she was in the passenger seat of his pickup while Sam was buckled in the backseat of the extended cab.

"I can't believe you brought your whole family to see my game, Lace! That was so cool! I had more people there than anybody!"

"They all wanted to come, Sam," Laci assured him. "It was fun. And you were great. I have a feeling you're the best one on the team."

"If I am, it's just 'cause Dad plays ball with me a lot. He teaches me all kinds of stuff."

That didn't surprise Laci. She had a feeling that Eric's priorities were right where they ought to be. He seemed to be a good Christian man, and he was trying to be the best parent he could be for his son. It appeared he was doing a wonderful job, too.

After Eric parked his pickup and they started walking toward the restaurant, Sam's hunger had him skipping a few steps ahead of them.

"It was nice of your family to show up, Laci," Eric said in a low voice. "For a minute there I thought Sam was going to be too nervous to play his normal game. But then you started cheering him on, and that was all it took. Thank you again."

"You're welcome." Just hearing her presence had that kind of effect on Sam caused Laci to wonder if she'd done the right thing by going. What if she didn't go the next time? How would that affect Sam?

As if he could read her thoughts, Eric said, "I know you won't be able to come to all his games, so please don't worry about it. He might be disappointed, but he'll always remember today."

The thought of Sam being disappointed in her saddened her deeply. "I'll try to make as many of his games as I can while I'm here," Laci said. Suddenly it dawned on her that her indecision about going back to Dallas might be a good thing at the moment. She could commit only to the present.

Sam pushed open the door to the Pizza Palace, and Laci and Eric hurried to catch up with him. Gram, Will, Sara, Jake, and Meggie were waiting for them at two tables that had been pulled together.

"Hi, Sam!" Meggie said. "You played good!"

"Thanks!" Sam claimed a chair beside her, leaving the two empty ones side by side for his dad and Laci.

Eric held out the chair for her, and for a moment Laci had a glimpse of what it would be like to be a threesome with him and Sam. And she liked the feeling.

"They have a buffet tonight," Jake said. "We told them we'd have six adults and two children, but we waited until you came to get started."

"Thanks," Eric said.

Will said the blessing, and then they all headed to the pizza bar to fill their plates.

"I want cheese pizza, Dad," Sam said. "And can I have that dessert pizza, too?"

"If you eat all this, okay?"

"Okay."

It took a few minutes before everyone was back at the table with their plates piled high with pizza.

"I do thank you all for coming to Sam's game," Eric said as his son and Meggie began eating. "It meant a lot to him."

"I'd forgotten how much fun it was to watch those little ones play ball," Will said. "I'd like to go again."

"He has games on Tuesday evenings and Saturday mornings. We'd love to have a cheering section whenever any of you can make it."

"You'll be seeing us there," Gram said.

"I've told Eric I'll make as many of Sam's games as I can. . . at least until I return to Dallas." Laci knew she would delay going back as long as she could. But she still wasn't sure what she should do, especially about her business.

"You just need to move home," Jake stated. "You don't want to go back. You know you don't."

"But, Jake, I do have a business there. And while my

assistant is taking care of everything while I'm gone, I have to decide what to do about it. If I move back here, it would mean giving up a clientele I worked hard to establish and starting all over again. Most of my business comes by word of mouth from one client recommending me to another." Laci shook her head. "I'm just not sure what I should be doing."

"I've told you what I think," Gram said. "I'd love for you to come home. You'd get a lot more word-of-mouth recommendations here at home than in a city like Dallas."

"Well, I did see a little house over on Fourth Street that I think would make a wonderful place to set up business in. I haven't actually looked at it, but I have been thinking about it. Maybe I need to mention it to Myra and see if she would want to take over managing the shop in Dallas or start her own business. And I could go to the bank and see what my options are."

"Maybe you could just open a consulting business here at first," Sara suggested.

"I can tell you this: Will and I have decided to keep my house and sell his once we're married. We will probably want to do some remodeling after we're married, to make the house more *ours*. We'd be more than happy to hire you and promote you, Laci. You know that."

"You lived here all your life until you moved to Dallas," Jake said. "You have a whole lot of people who would probably come to you for help. There aren't many interior decorators around here."

Laci knew she should have realized that before she moved to Dallas. Love for her family swelled. They would help her establish her business here. . .and they would have then. What had she been thinking when she moved away? But what meant the most was that they truly seemed to want her to move back.

"Thank you all. I guess it wouldn't hurt to look at that house. I'm sure it would need some work to turn it into a shop."

"Well, Eric could help you with that," Sara said.

Laci turned to Eric. "Would you mind taking a look at it with me?"

"I'd be glad to. I love building new homes, but I really love working with older ones. Just let me know when."

"I'll call the Realtor tomorrow and find out when I can see it."

"Just give me a call and I'll meet you there," Eric said, pulling a card out of his wallet and handing it to her. "Most of the time it's easier to reach me on my cell phone, so you might want to try it first."

"Thanks, Eric." Laci took the card but wasn't prepared for the jolt that shot up her arm and straight to her heart at the brush of his fingertips on hers. She slipped the card into her purse with trembling fingers. What was it about this man that had her reacting like she was in high school again? Yes, she'd had a crush on him, but that was years ago and she'd gotten over it. Or had she? Was she trying to relive the past, or was this something entirely different? She didn't know. She loved being back in Sweet Springs, but she'd never been more confused about everything in her life than she was at this minute.

❧

They were nearly through eating before Eric got up the nerve to bring up the movies as Jake had suggested out at the ballpark.

"There's a movie I've been wanting to see at the new six-screen theater," he said in a low tone, hoping only Laci heard him. "Jake says he and Sara will be glad to watch Sam tonight if you'd like to go with me." He told her the name of it. "It's supposed to be really good."

It took Laci a moment to answer as she had to swallow the bite she was chewing. Eric's heart seemed to stop beating while he waited. He would let Jake have it if she refused.

"I've heard it is. I'd love to go." She smiled at him. "What time is the next showing?"

He breathed an inward sigh of relief that she hadn't turned him down, and his heart began to beat again—hard and strong. He looked at his watch. "It starts in about forty minutes."

"Okay." She smiled and nodded. "Sounds great."

Eric looked over at Jake. "We're going to the seven-thirty showing if you and Sara are still sure you don't mind watching Sam tonight."

"Are you kidding?" Sara asked. "Meggie will love having the company!"

"I'll be by to pick him up as soon as the show is over."

"Not a problem," Jake said.

The next thirty minutes passed in a blur for Eric. Sam had been happy to go home with Jake and Sara to play with Meggie and waved good-bye with a grin. By the time Eric and Laci took their seats in the movie theater, he still couldn't believe he'd asked her out or that she'd agreed to go with him.

Something about sitting in the darkened theater had a cozy feel to him. But with Laci sitting beside him, he felt like a teenager on his first date. He wasn't quite sure how to act.

"I haven't been to the movies in a while," he whispered to her while the upcoming movies were being advertised.

"Neither have I," she said. "This is a very nice theater. I'm so glad Sweet Springs is growing the way it is. It's kept its small-town feel, though, and I'm happy about that."

"So am I." Eric was thankful she seemed at ease. Maybe his nervousness wasn't too apparent. But as the movie started he truly did feel like a teenager again. It was hard to concentrate on what was happening on the screen when all he could think about was if he should put his arm around Laci, try to hold her hand, or just sit there like they were mere acquaintances.

He certainly didn't like the latter thought. But putting his arm around her might seem a little too familiar. Finally he reached out and grasped her hand lightly in his. It was only when her fingers curved around his own that Eric relaxed and began to enjoy the movie.

When it was over and the lights came back on in the theater, he gave Laci's fingers a squeeze before letting go. "Thank you for coming with me. I really enjoyed that."

"So did I," Laci said as they made their way up the aisle. "Thank you for asking me."

He looked at his watch. He hated for the evening to end yet. Jake had told him he didn't have to hurry back right after the show. "Would you like to grab a cup of coffee or something?"

"I'd love to."

"Let's go to the ice-cream parlor downtown. They make good cappuccino."

"That sounds great."

It took only a few minutes to get back downtown, and soon they were standing at the counter in the old-fashioned ice-cream parlor. After looking at the selections they both ordered a frozen cappuccino and took them to one of the tables outside. The moon was bright, and the sky was filled with stars that looked so close he could almost reach out and touch one.

"Oh, how nice it is out here," Laci said. "This wasn't open when I left home."

"I guess it wasn't. It's a very popular spot this time of year. But it does a good business all year long. They serve hot chocolate and all kinds of specialty coffees, too."

"Mmm, that will be nice."

"Laci, your family sure would like you to move back home." He didn't add that he would like for her to do that also.

"I know."

"Do you think you will?"

"I don't know. I"—she broke off and shook her head—"I just don't know what I'm going to do."

Eric's heart sank. Attracted as he was to Laci, he needed to step back. It would do no good to fall in love with her if she was going back to Dallas to stay. No good at all.

The evening didn't end quite the way Eric would have liked it to. He would like to have known Laci was moving back. Would probably have asked her out again. But with her not knowing what she was going to do, he decided to take a wait-and-see attitude. That didn't stop him from wanting to kiss her good night when he walked her to the door, though.

But he didn't. Instead, he just thanked her again for going with him.

"I had a good time. Thank you for taking me," she said.

"Well, I guess we'll see you later. Be sure to call me about meeting you at the house if you decide to look at it." He hoped she would.

"I will."

Eric stepped off the porch. "Tell your grandmother thank you again for coming to Sam's game."

"I will."

" 'Night."

"Good night, Eric," Laci said before slipping inside the house.

He headed for his truck feeling even more like a teenager than ever.

❧

When he picked up Sam, he didn't give Jake a chance to ask much about the evening.

"How'd it go?" his friend asked.

"Real good. It was a great movie," Eric told him as he tried to hurry out the door. "I'd better get this little guy home. Thank you both so much."

"Anytime," Sara said, standing beside Jake to see them out. "We mean that, too."

"Thank you," Eric said. "See you later."

It felt a little lonely as he and Sam took off for home.

"Was the movie good, Dad?"

"It was."

"It was fun at the pizza place, wasn't it?"

"It sure was, son." In fact, spending the evening with Laci and the others had been as enjoyable as the past Sunday afternoon had been—up to the point he'd asked her about moving back here.

"I hope we can do it again. Do you think Lace will come to the game on Saturday?"

"She said she would. You know, Sam, Laci lives in Dallas. She came home because her grandmother was so sick, and now she's staying to help her. She'll probably be going back to Texas one of these days."

"Maybe she'll move back here. I heard everyone talking about it."

Eric had no doubt his son had heard every word spoken at the table. "Well, she might decide to do that. Then again she might not."

"I'm gonna pray she moves back."

Eric didn't want to discourage his son's prayer life, but he had to prepare him for being disappointed. "You can do that. But remember—sometimes what we want isn't what God thinks is best. And He always knows what is best."

Sam nodded. "I know."

Eric let out a deep breath. He had some praying to do, too.

After Sam showered, Eric listened to his prayers, and, true to his word, Sam prayed about Laci.

"Dear God, thank You for Dad and for all my blessings. Thank You for letting me do good at T-ball today. And please let Lace decide to move back here. In Jesus' name, amen."

Eric kissed his son on the forehead. " 'Night, son. I love you."

"I love you, too, Dad."

Eric went back to the utility room, pulled out a pile of wrinkled towels and washcloths from the dryer, and took them to the kitchen table. He was sure glad it wasn't full of wrinkled clothes he'd have to iron. As he began to fold the bath towels, he thought back over the evening. He wondered if Laci felt the same shock of electricity he had when he handed her his card. He'd been totally surprised by his reaction to her.

Something about Laci drew him to her. Maybe it was the way she was so gentle and kind to Sam. She'd been sweet and pretty in high school, but she'd grown into a caring and lovely woman who had his heart thumping double time in his chest when she smiled at him—and had him trying to figure out how to ask her out again. Even after tonight and not knowing what she was going to do, he wanted to spend more time with her. Yet, if she didn't move back here, what future could there be?

Sam wasn't the only one hoping Laci would move back home. But until then Eric needed to be careful not to lose his heart to her and especially to guard Sam against caring too much for her, as well. The last thing either of them needed was more heartache in their lives. Eric sat down at the table and bowed his head. It was his turn to pray.

"Dear Lord, I thank You for all my blessings here on this earth. . .especially for Sam. Like him, I ask that if it is Your will, Laci will move back here. But, Lord, if it's not, please guard our hearts. Please help me to know what You'd have me do where Laci is concerned. I don't know whether to pursue a relationship with her or keep my distance. So please show me, Lord. Thank You most of all for Your plan for our salvation through Your Son, Jesus Christ. In His precious name I pray, amen."

He'd come to count on the Lord more each day after his wife's death. He'd continue to leave things in His hands.

❧

Laci found it hard to get to sleep that night with so many thoughts running through her mind fighting to be heard. She'd enjoyed going to the movie with Eric. He seemed to be having a good time, too, until he brought her home. She wasn't sure what had been going through his mind when he'd walked her to the door. He'd seemed quieter after he'd asked her if she was moving. She just hadn't known how to answer him. Deep down inside she knew she wanted to come home. But she'd wanted to move to Dallas at one time, too. She'd been wrong then. Was she right now? Was it what she *should* do? That was the big question.

There was no denying that, while being closer to family was the biggest reason for wanting to move back, the fact that Eric and his son lived here had a lot to do with it, too. Yet was that wise? She was very attracted to Eric, and Sam had already claimed a spot in her heart. But he needed a mother, and she just didn't know—and *why* was she thinking about this anyway? Eric hadn't let her know how he felt about her. Just because he'd taken her to the movie or held her hand didn't mean he truly cared. And just because her pulse raced each time she was near him didn't mean his did. She could be weaving those high school dreams all over again, with the same results—that Eric didn't feel the same way about her.

If she did move home was she just letting herself in for heartache? And yet the thought of going back to Dallas, not being able to have daily contact with her loved ones, not having the hope of running into Eric and Sam, to move through her days and nights instead of enjoying them, made Laci shudder. She wasn't sure she could go back to the boring life she had lived in Texas.

Finally, after tossing and turning, she got out of bed and went to sit on the window seat in her room. Gazing out at the multitude of stars in the sky, David's lesson on giving things over to the Lord finally came to mind.

Maybe her problems had been from lack of doing that in the past, Laci realized. Not only had she not listened to her family's advice, she couldn't remember ever going to the Lord in prayer over her decision to move to Dallas.

Nor had she gone to Him for much while she was there. She'd been so busy concentrating on what *she* wanted that she'd forgotten to ask the Lord what *He* wanted her to do. Even since she'd been home, she'd been doing much the same thing, except she was more confused than she'd ever been in her life and needed to take things to the Lord. But had she done it? No. Well, no wonder she stayed confused over everything. Somewhere along the way she'd forgotten it was the Lord's will she was to be doing and not her own.

The realization of how long and how much she'd been putting her wants first brought Laci onto her knees at the window seat, tears streaming down her face as she went to the Lord in prayer.

"Dear Father, please forgive me for blindly forging ahead with my life and leaving You out of the decision making. For not coming to You in prayer and asking Your guidance for my future. Please forgive me for drifting away from the committed Christian I once was and help me to grow as Your child. Please guide me now and help me make the right decision about coming home or staying in Dallas and about everything else in my life. Please help me seek Your will in all of this, Father. Thank You for the many blessings You've given me, especially for Your Son, Jesus. In His name I pray, amen."

Laci truly felt as if a load had been lifted off her shoulders when she finished praying. She went back to bed and drifted off to sleep in only minutes.

The next morning she was still not sure what the Lord wanted her to do, but she trusted He would let her know in due time. She called the Realtor and set up an appointment for her and Eric to look at the house. She was pleased and surprised to find the Realtor was a young woman she'd gone to school with. Her name had been Jeanette Williams in school, but her married name was Fielding.

"Laci, I'm busy with another client this morning, but I'll be glad to show it to you around two this afternoon," Jeanette said. "Will that work for you?"

"That will be fine. I'll meet you there," Laci said.

She had been nervous about calling Eric afterward, but he'd been very nice and had agreed to meet them at the house at two that afternoon.

Jeanette was there waiting when Laci arrived at the house, and Eric pulled up right behind her.

"Eric, how nice to see you," Jeanette said. "I didn't know. . . are you two looking at this for yourselves?"

"I—uh—yes—no." Laci wasn't sure how to answer her. She felt a little embarrassed at the question.

Eric came to her rescue. "I'm going to give Laci advice on anything that might need to be done to the house, should she decide to lease or buy it."

"Oh, I see." Jeanette nodded and smiled at Laci as they reached the front porch. "Eric and I have worked together some in the past. I've sold a couple of homes he's built. He'll give you great advice."

"That's what I'm counting on."

Jeanette unlocked the front door and stood to the side for them to enter the house.

"Ohh, this is wonderful," Laci said when she walked through the front door. The hardwood floors were in excellent condition, at least in the front of the house. The bay window, in what would have been the parlor, was beautiful and gave plenty of light to the room. The kitchen and dining room were also downstairs. Upstairs were two large bedrooms and a bathroom. It was just the right size for her needs.

"This area is zoned commercial, isn't it?" she asked Jeanette as they came back downstairs.

"Yes, it is. What were you thinking of using the property for?"

"I'm an interior decorator and have a business in Dallas. But I'm thinking of moving back and opening up a shop here."

"Oh, how wonderful, Laci! We could use a good decorator in this town," Jeanette said. "Sweet Springs has grown in the last few years. I'd think you'd have all the work you might want right here."

Laci hoped so, if she did move. That was still something she was waiting for the Lord to show her. She just needed to learn how to be still and listen.

ten

After they left Jeanette at the house with the promise that Laci would be in touch with her, Laci and Eric went to the diner for coffee. There was a lull in business at that time of day, and Dee was in a talkative mood when she brought the coffee and pie they'd ordered to the table. "Hey, what have you two been up to today?"

"I went to look at a piece of property. I'm thinking about buying or leasing it, if possible, to use for my business—if I decide to move back. I asked Eric if he would give me his opinion on it."

"Makes sense to me. I hope you do move back," Dee said then abruptly changed the subject. "Have you heard from John or your parents on how his campaign is going lately?"

"No. Not since they were here this past weekend." Laci noticed a light in Dee's eyes, prompting her to ask, "Have you heard from him?"

"Yeah, I did. He called here a little while ago. I'm. . .not sure why. But anyway he said the campaign is going well."

"Did he say when he was coming back home for a few days?"

Dee shook her head. "I was so surprised he'd called that I didn't think to ask. He did ask how things were going here."

"Oh?" Laci wasn't sure what to ask next. It was obvious Dee was pleased John had called her, but she seemed a little flustered by it.

The bell rang over the door, and Dee seemed somewhat

relieved to be able to say, "Got to go. I'll be back with a coffee refill in a little while."

"That was odd," Laci said when Dee left their table.

"Didn't she and John date at one time?"

"Yes, they did. But as far as I know they're just friends now." She almost told him her family thought John and Dee still cared about each other but decided against it. Changing the subject, she asked, "What did you think of the house?"

"It's a jewel. The house is in wonderful shape, Laci. I'm not sure how much room you'd need for your shop or if you want to keep the kitchen intact. I'd advise you to keep a kitchen downstairs, in case you ever wanted to sell the house, but we could remodel it pretty much however you want to. The house was built to last and has been well taken care of."

"That's what I wanted to hear. I'm not sure about what I'd want to change if I do take it. I think I could use it like it is, for a while anyway."

"Just keep in mind it would be much easier to do any re-modeling before you move in than after. It can be a real mess."

Laci nodded. "You're right. Do you have any suggestions?"

"Well, first I need to know how you envision using the space." Eric forked a piece of peach pie into his mouth.

"I thought at first of making an apartment upstairs. But I can see that might hurt the resale value if I did want to sell it later on. I think I could still live there, though. One of the bedrooms could be a living room, and I could still use the kitchen downstairs. The dining room could become my office space and workroom while the living area could be a reception area where I first meet with clients. I could furnish it in keeping with the time period in which the house was built." The more she talked about it, the better it sounded.

"That sounds great, Laci. You might want to think about

putting in a small powder room under the stairwell so you or your clients wouldn't have to run upstairs."

"Oh, that's a wonderful idea, Eric."

"Hidden there, it wouldn't take away from the historical feel of the house. If you'd like, I can draw up a plan for the powder room for you—no charge, of course."

"Thank you, Eric. I'd like to see what you have in mind. But I'd be glad to pay you."

"Nah. I may need your advice on decorating Sam's room one of these days. He wants something to do with baseball. We can swap services."

"It's a deal. I'd love to come up with something for Sam's room."

"He'd love that. Other than the powder room it doesn't look as if you'll need to do much remodeling, so that will hold down the cost for you. I'm sure you're capable of decorating it to suit your needs." He grinned at her.

"I would hope so. Otherwise I'm in the wrong business."

"Does this mean you've decided to move here?"

"I'm still not sure—"

"You really ought to do it, Laci. Your family wants you to. Take it from me. Family is too precious to take for granted."

Suddenly Laci felt as if he were criticizing her. And who was he to tell her what to do, just because she'd asked for his advice about the house? "I'm not taking my family for granted! But I haven't made up my mind yet. It's just too important a decision to make in a hurry."

"I didn't mean to—" Eric's cell phone rang just then, and he answered it. After a quick conversation he pulled some bills out of his wallet and put them on the table. "I've got to run. There's a problem at one of the home sites I'm building. I have to check it out. Laci, I didn't mean to make you mad. I—"

"Don't worry about it." Laci knew she sounded cool, but it hurt to think he felt she didn't care about her family.

"Well. . .thanks for asking me to take a look at the house."

"Eric, you did me a favor." She handed him back the money he left on the table. "I'll get our ticket."

"Nope. I'll get it." He put the bills back on the table. "I'll talk to you later, okay?"

"Sure." Did he mean he'd call? Or just that they'd run into each other? Laci didn't know, and she hated for the afternoon to end on this note. But maybe it was best this way.

❧

The next day was the meeting of the Wedding Planners, Inc., and this time they piled in Sara's SUV and headed for Roswell to look at wedding dresses and see if anything appealed to Gram.

"Well, even if I don't find anything, these outings with you girls are fun," Gram said. "I don't dare choose anything today. Lydia would be upset with me if I did. I'll have to wait on her. But at least this way I'll have a better idea of what I'm looking at when I see them in the magazines."

"That's true. It's hard to feel the material in a picture," Aunt Nora said. "And there are very few pictures of flower girl dresses. Maybe we can find something for Meggie."

They stopped at one of their favorite Mexican restaurants for lunch before going to look at dresses. It was then Laci told them about John calling Dee.

"He did? Hmm," Sara said. "Did Dee seem surprised?"

"Yes, she did—and a bit flustered. But she also seemed happy."

"Maybe he's doing some thinking out there on that campaign trail."

"Could be someone mentioned that Richard Tyler has been

seen spending a lot of time at the diner," Rae said.

"Oh? Who would that be?" Aunt Nora asked.

"Luke might have mentioned it to him."

"Well, is it true?" Gram asked.

"Luke wouldn't lie. We've seen Richard in there. 'Course I don't know if he's making a play for Dee or not, but he's been there."

"You two aren't playing matchmaker, are you?"

"Oh, no one in this family does that, do they, Gram?" Sara asked then chuckled.

The laughter around the table had Laci looking at them curiously. "Just how much matchmaking does this family do?"

"Oh, we've been known to do a little on occasion," Aunt Nora said with a laugh.

"On several occasions, you mean," Gram said. "You'd love to have been in on it, Laci. Neither Sara nor Rae would be family now if it hadn't been for a little matchmaking."

"Is that true?" Laci looked from Sara to Rae.

"Oh, yeah, it is. And Dee got in on some of it herself. It's only fair if we do the same to her."

"I'd love to see her and John together," Laci said. "You don't think we're reading more into this than there is, though, do you?"

"Not if John called her, I don't," Rae said. "That was what Luke was hoping for. I can't wait to tell him."

Laci couldn't help but laugh. She hoped it worked out so no one was hurt. Dee looked so happy the day before.

By the time they arrived at the bridal shop they decided they should have gone there first.

"I feel stuffed," Gram said. "It was those sopaipillas and honey that did it. I don't think I want to try on anything today, but I still want to look. Just remind me next time not to eat before we come here."

They spent the better part of the afternoon oohing and aahing over dresses and colors. They saw dresses in Meggie's size, and she was ready and willing to try them on. Each one looked pretty on her, and she wanted them all.

"Well, Meggie, my love, at least we know we'll find a beautiful outfit for you. We just need to find out what colors Gram wants, and we'll know where to come," Aunt Nora said as they left the shop.

It was a delightful afternoon, and Laci prayed it would be the Lord's will for her to spend many more with this wonderful family of hers.

&

When Will came over that evening, Gram was excited to tell him about the afternoon and even had some magazines out to ask his opinion about a few things. Laci figured they could use a little time to themselves and decided to go to the diner to visit with Dee, if she had time.

She went upstairs to get her purse, and when she came back downstairs Gram was just getting off the phone. "Oh, dear, I thought you'd already left. Sara said to tell you to call her later."

"Okay. I'll call on my cell phone. I won't be late." She gave her grandmother a kiss on the cheek and gave Will a kiss, too, on the way out the door. He looked a little bewildered with all those bridal magazines spread out before him.

She stepped into her car and punched in Jake and Sara's number before she backed out of the drive. When Sara answered, she said, "Hi. Gram said I was supposed to call you?"

"Oh, yes, Laci, we need to start planning her shower. Did we decide to meet at the diner?"

"Yes, Dee wanted to help, remember?"

"Okay. Gram said you were on your way there. Ask Dee what afternoon will work best for her and let the rest of us know, okay? I hate to call her at work; she's usually so busy."

"I'll check with her and get back to you."

"Good. Oh, and see if you can find out if John has called her again. Luke and Jake have been doing a lot of calling. I think they *are* up to something."

Laci laughed. "Okay, I'll see what I can find out. Talk to you later."

Several customers were in the diner when Laci got there, but they were nearly finished eating and Annie was working, so Dee was able to chat for a few minutes.

"I talked to Sara, and we decided we need to start planning that shower for Gram. What day and time would be best for you to meet?"

"Midmornings on most days are pretty good. And on Fridays I usually have extra help, so how about ten thirty tomorrow? Is that too short a notice?"

"I don't think so. Let me check with the others, and I'll let you know."

After three quick calls they had it set for the next morning, and Laci was excited to start the planning. "Gram is going to be so surprised."

"If anyone deserves something special, it's your grand-mother. She's a really fine lady," Dee said. "What kind of shower are we giving? She probably doesn't need a lot of things for her home."

"I don't know. We'll see what the others think."

The bell over the door signaled new customers, and Laci's heart fluttered in her chest at the sight of Eric and Sam coming in.

"Well, hi, guys," Dee said. "You just left here a little while ago. Did you forget something?"

"Nah. Dad just said we needed a treat and asked if I wanted a milkshake—and for no reason. Can you believe it?" Sam climbed up on the stool beside Laci. "Hi, Lace! Are you having a milkshake, too?"

"Hi, Sam. No, this is cherry limeade. But a shake sure sounds good."

"I'll have a chocolate one, please," Sam said to Dee, sounding much older than five.

"I'll have strawberry," Eric said.

"Okay," Dee said. "Coming right up."

"I still can't believe Dad is going to let me have one. He usually saves them for special occasions."

Eric shrugged. "We've been cleaning house. It just sounded good."

Laci laughed. "It's fun to be spontaneous sometimes, isn't it?"

"What's spon–tan–e–us?" Sam asked.

"It's what I did tonight. Like deciding to do something all of a sudden," Eric said.

"Oh, okay. Yeah, it is fun! Is that what you did, Lace?"

Laci shook her head. "Not really. I just decided to come visit with Dee awhile."

"And give your grandmother and Will some time to themselves?" Eric asked.

"How did you know?"

He shook his head. "I just guessed. It's something you'd do."

At least he seemed to realize she did care about her grandmother. Maybe she'd taken his words the wrong way the other day. She hoped so.

Dee came back with the milkshakes for Eric and Sam, and Laci remembered she was supposed to find out if she'd talked to John again.

"I haven't heard from Mom or Dad or John in days, and I haven't been able to get in touch with them. They must be in an area where their cell phone signals are weak. Have you heard anymore, Dee?"

Dee turned almost the color of Eric's strawberry milkshake. "As a matter of fact, John did call this afternoon. I think they may be coming in soon for a few days."

"Okay, good." Laci could tell Dee was a little flustered so she tried to sound nonchalant. "I hope so because I know Gram would like Mom's opinion on a few things."

More customers came in, and she could tell Dee was relieved not to have to talk about John anymore as she hurried to wait on them. But it appeared something was up. She just didn't have a clue as to what.

"How's practice been going?" she asked Sam.

"Good. Do you think you—"

"Sam. Remember what we talked about?"

"Yes, sir. I'm sorry, Lace. Dad said not to make you feel like you *have* to come to my games. And that you might be going back to Dallas, so I shouldn't get my hopes up." He let out a huge sigh.

Laci's heart twisted inside at Sam's words and the look in his eyes. She had to find a way to make him feel better. "Sam, what your dad said was true. I may be going back to Dallas. I'm just not sure yet. But while I am here, I intend to be at your games, okay?"

"Okay!"

Her gaze met Eric's over the top of his son's head, and he mouthed a "Thank you" to her. She nodded and smiled.

❧

Laci didn't know who was more surprised the next morning when she and Aunt Nora and Sara and Rae got to the diner to find her brother John sitting at the counter talking to Dee.

"When did you get into town, big brother? You could have let us know you were coming. Did Mom and Dad come back in, too?"

"Hi, sis!" John stood and gave her and the others hugs. "We got in late last night. We went to a fund-raising event in Ruidoso and left when it was over. But you're right—we should have let you know. I guess we aren't used to you being here in Sweet Springs, Laci. I came in to have breakfast before I check on things at the office, and then I need to get over to campaign headquarters."

It sounded as if Jake didn't know he was there, and from Sara's reaction to seeing him, Laci was pretty sure she didn't either. She didn't think anyone knew they were coming back, but that didn't make her feel better. "Yes, well, I need to call Mom. We're starting to plan Gram's shower, and I think she might want to be in on it."

She left the others talking to John as she stepped outside to get a good signal and punched in the numbers. She felt kind of grouchy, and she didn't even know why. Maybe because she had a feeling that if she were in Dallas instead of here, she would know nothing about what was going on. She wouldn't be in on planning the wedding or the shower, she wouldn't know when her parents and John were in or out of town, and she would be missing out on the suspense with Dee and her brother. But she couldn't blame her parents and brother for having to get used to letting her know these things. Eventually they would, *if* she moved back to stay.

She took a deep breath when her mother answered the phone and tried not to sound as frustrated and confused as she felt. "Hey, Mom. I just met up with John at the diner. Aunt Nora and the rest of us are here to start planning Gram's shower.

I thought you might want to meet us—"

"I'll be there in twenty minutes, dear," her mother assured her. "I tried to call you last night and let you know we were coming in, but Mom's line was busy, and I couldn't get through to you either."

Feeling slightly mollified, Laci felt herself begin to relax. "I'm glad you're here. We'll be waiting for you."

She joined the other women at the big round booth in the front corner and tried not to notice the high color in Dee's face as she brought them coffee.

"I'll be right with you," she said.

"Mom won't be here for another fifteen minutes or so, Dee. It's okay," Laci tried to reassure her. But from watching her reaction to John and the way he kept looking at Dee, she had to believe they might be on the verge of discovering how much they still cared about each other. They probably just needed a big gentle push.

eleven

"Those two love each other, or I am blind as a bat," Aunt Nora said as they watched Dee and John stealing glances.

"I've thought that for a long time," Rae said. "And Dee told me they dated at one time, but that was all. She shut up like a clam after that."

"They did date," Sara said. "But something happened, and they broke up. I'm not sure anyone in the family knows why."

"Well, they might have broken up with each other, but it doesn't look to me as if they ever fell out of love," Aunt Nora said.

Laci didn't think so either. "There's something very caring in their expressions when they look at each other. How can everyone else see what Dee and John don't seem to?"

"Well, all I can tell you is that Jake and Luke are up to something, and Rae and I think they are doing some matchmaking," Sara said.

"They would," Aunt Nora said. "Those two are so happily married; they want John to have the same thing. I hope whatever they're planning works. Tell them if they need any help I'll be glad to assist."

Laci's mom arrived and slipped into the booth beside her. "Hey, darlin'. It's so good to have you here in Sweet Springs."

John walked over to tell them good-bye when he left to go to the office, and if he felt five pairs of eyes on his back, waiting to see if he talked to Dee, he didn't let on. He did say something that had Dee blushing when he paid his ticket, and even Laci's mom had to comment.

"That boy is bright, and he's going to make an excellent senator. But when it comes to his love life he doesn't seem to have a clue. Those two have been mooning over each other for years now. If he doesn't act pretty soon or she doesn't give him some encouragement, I don't see much hope for either of them ever getting married."

Dee headed over to join them, and the topic quickly turned to Gram's shower plans. By lunchtime they'd set a date, a time, and a place. Since Gram knew so many people in town, they decided to use the fellowship hall at church and send out invitations to make sure the shower stayed a secret. And they would enlist the aid of the Teddy Bear Brigade. It would be great.

The diner began to get busy, and Dee went back to work. Sara had to leave to pick up Meggie, but the rest of them decided to stay and have lunch since the smells wafting from the kitchen had stirred up their appetites. Besides, they'd only had coffee and tea, and they figured they'd give Dee their business.

"I think we'll have a huge turnout," Laci's mom said as they waited on their orders to arrive. "Everyone loves Mother. I can't wait to see her face. And after next week we'll be around awhile. Ben has some things to take care of at the ranch, and I want to help with the wedding plans. I mean, it's not every day a daughter gets to help her mother plan a wedding."

"Well, I'm glad to hear it," Aunt Nora said. "Ellie promised she'd let you in on the final decisions, and she meant it. She hasn't decided on anything. Your being here will speed up things. But we really need to get them to set a wedding date."

"I'll work on that. I know they'd like to wait until after the election, but that's not until November. Once we settle everything I'll feel better about going out and campaigning for John."

"You've been stressing, Mom?" Laci figured she had been. Her mother wanted to take care of everyone at once, and that was hard to do.

"I have been. I want to be with John. I want to spend time with you, and ever since Mother's stroke I want to spend more time with her."

Laci hugged her mother. "I know."

"I think we all want Will and Ellie married as soon as possible. They've been almost as bad as Dee and John." Aunt Nora shook her head. "Except they haven't been denying how they feel about each other."

"Well, once we have Mom and Will married, maybe we can concentrate on John and Dee," Laci's mom said.

For a moment Laci felt left out. She wouldn't mind their doing a little matchmaking on her behalf, especially because she had a feeling she'd messed up everything by being so short with Eric when he'd given her his opinion about moving home. She'd had some time to think, and she realized that maybe she was upset because Eric hadn't asked her to move back because *he* wanted to.

ະ

The next morning Laci and most of her family were at Sam's game cheering for him again. The smile on his face when he spotted them in the stands was something Laci knew she'd never forget. The game was tighter this time, but Sam and his friend Larry managed to keep their team afloat. Once again they won.

"You came! I knew you would," Sam said as he ran up to her and hugged her after the game.

"I told you I would."

"I know. And I prayed you'd be here. And you are." He turned to her family. "Thanks for coming, everyone."

Laci could tell her family was touched by his appreciation of them.

"I can't think of a better way to spend a Saturday morning, young man," Will said.

"Nor I," Gram said. "And now that we're out and about, I'm going to get Will to drive me to Roswell to do some shopping and take me to lunch."

" 'Bye, Gram. See you two later," Laci said.

"We're having lunch at the diner, Lace," Sam said. "Will you come with us?"

"Oh, I don't know, Sam. I'm sure your dad has plans—"

"We'd both love to have lunch with you, Laci. I just need to do a little cleanup here and talk to some of the parents. Can we meet you there in about thirty minutes?"

"Please, Lace!"

"Sure, that sounds good to me. I'll see you there, okay, Sam?"

"Okay!"

Laci took off for downtown with a smile in her heart, looking forward to having lunch with the two Mitchell men. She was planning to go to the diner anyway, but eating alone had never been her favorite thing.

When she arrived she found her brother at a table, about half finished with what looked like a late breakfast. Somehow that didn't surprise her, but she wondered how often he visited the diner when he was in town.

"Hey, sis! Sit down and keep me company."

Laci took a seat at the table for four, and Dee came over with a cup of coffee. "What can I get you, Laci?"

"I'll just have the coffee for now and order in a little while, Dee."

"Okay, just let me know when. John, you need a refill?"

"Yes, please, Dee." He smiled at her and nodded at an empty chair. "It's not real busy right now. Why don't you join us?"

"I might grab a cup," Dee said. But the bell over the door jingled then, and two different couples came in. "Well, maybe not. Looks like things are picking up." She sighed and shook her head as she went to wait on one couple while Annie took the other.

"She works way too hard," John said.

"She does," Laci agreed.

"I wish she'd just—" John stopped midsentence. "What are you up to this morning, sis?"

"Some of the family and I went to Sam Mitchell's T-ball game, and he and Eric asked me to have lunch with them."

"Oh?" John raised his eyebrow. "Something going on I ought to know about?"

Laci wished she could say yes. But the truth was the truth. "No. Not that I know of. Sam has taken a liking to me, and when the family found out he had no one to root for him at the games we all decided to go cheer him on."

"Uh-huh. I seem to remember you had a crush on Eric when you were in high school." John had that ornery big-brother grin on his face. "He's a good man."

Laci could feel the ornery little-sister response coming. "Yeah, well, it was a crush. We never actually dated—like you and Dee did. What's up with the two of you?"

"What do you mean?" John asked a bit defensively.

"John, the only place I've seen you since you've been home is here."

"So? I eat here a lot. It's close to the office."

Laci shook her head. "I don't think that's the reason you come here so often."

"What are you talking about, sis?"

"Oh, John, anyone watching the two of you together can see you and Dee both still care about each other."

"We're good friends. Of course we care about each other."

"You know what I mean."

"No, I don't." John took a sip of his coffee and stood, pulling bills out of his wallet. "And I don't have time to find out. I'm about to be late to a meeting. See you later, sis. Love you." He bent and kissed her on the cheek before striding toward the cash register.

Trying not to be obvious, Laci watched him as he paid Dee. He smiled and leaned over and murmured something to Dee, and she nodded and smiled back. Something about the way those two looked at each other was almost tangible. Anyone watching could see they cared about each other—deeply.

Laci watched her brother leave the diner and Dee go back to waiting on customers, wondering if either of them would ever admit it. She sipped her coffee for a few minutes, almost wishing she hadn't brought it up to John. Now he would probably avoid her for a few days at least. He knew she was right. He hadn't wanted to talk about his relationship with Dee. If he felt only friendship for her, as he said, he wouldn't have been so defensive.

Of course, she'd been a little on the defensive when he'd mentioned Eric, Laci reminded herself. So who was she to be upset at her brother for doing the same?

"Lace, we're here!" Sam said as he barreled into the diner and up to the table where she was sitting.

"Hey, Sam, I bet you're starving by now."

"I *am* hungry." He climbed up in the chair John had vacated.

"So am I," Eric said, taking the chair on the other side of Laci.

When Dee came to clear John's dishes away and get their order, it took only a minute to give it. Sam wanted his usual, but Laci and Eric chose hamburgers and fries.

&.

Eric let his son have Laci's full attention for a few minutes as they rehashed the game and talked about how well he had played. But once Dee came back with their orders and Sam began eating, he took his turn at claiming her attention. "I saw John on his way down to the office. Is he going to be in town long?"

Laci sighed. "I don't know. I should have asked, but I think he's a little aggravated at me at the moment."

"Oh? What happened?"

She sighed. "Big brother that he is, he started teasing me about an old crush I had when I was in high school, and I couldn't resist firing back at him."

Eric chuckled. "I seem to remember you always gave as good as you got when he or your cousins teased you. What did you say?"

"Oh, I mentioned the fact that he and Dee had actually dated in high school and it was obvious they still cared about each other."

"I bet he wasn't too happy about that. John never has liked talking much about his personal life."

"No, he wasn't happy." Laci sighed and shook her head. "He didn't want to talk about it. But I hit a nerve. I know I did. Still, I should have kept my mouth shut. If they were getting to the point of admitting how they feel, I sure hope I didn't set things back."

"I don't think it will hurt things, Laci. I've been watching them a long time, and you're right. They care. Who knows? Maybe you gave him the push he needs."

"I doubt it. But I sure hope someone will."

A nice-looking man came in and sat at the counter. From Dee's reaction to him it appeared he wasn't a favorite of hers, but the man seemed to like her a lot. "Do you know who that man is?"

Eric nodded. "His name is Richard Tyler. He's been trying to get Dee to go out with him for a while now."

"Oh, I see." Laci began to chuckle.

"What's so funny?"

"I think my cousins are using him to spur John into action."

"What? Ohh. . ." Eric nodded and grinned. "Well, maybe that's the push that will do it."

"And now I can say I saw him in here, too—maybe ask John about him."

"Well, after your conversation with him today, is it possible he might think you're trying to get a reaction out of him?"

"Oh, you're right. He probably would. I guess I'll have to be careful about what I say to him for a while."

"Probably. But—maybe I could find a way to work it into a conversation."

Laci nodded, and her smile widened. She patted him on the arm. "I like the way you think, Eric."

A jolt of electricity shot up his arm at her touch. Eric hoped that wasn't all she liked about him, because he could no longer deny he was falling deeply in love with Laci Tanner. "Dad. . . Dad!" Sam said. "Can I have the ketchup, please?"

"Oh, yes." He handed the ketchup to his son as he tried to come to grips with what he'd just admitted to himself. And he might be the only one who knew how he felt. He didn't know if he'd ever be able to tell Laci. He didn't have any idea how she felt about him, other than as a friend. Nor did he know if she was going to return to Dallas or move back to Sweet

Springs. And after the way she reacted when he'd given her his opinion about that, he wasn't in any hurry to upset her again. At least she didn't seem angry with him anymore. What he did know was she had a claim on his heart, and how she felt about him or where she lived or didn't live probably wouldn't make any difference in how he felt about her.

He wondered if John was going through the same feelings about Dee, and he could suddenly sympathize with him.

"Eric? Are you all right?" Laci asked, pulling him out of his thoughts. "You looked miles away for a moment."

He chuckled. "No, I'm right here. I'm fine." Or he would be—with the Lord's help. "I'll try to figure out a way to mention old Richard over there to John. Maybe Sam and I will stop by his campaign headquarters later today."

"That might work," Laci said.

"Yes, we need a yard sign for John's campaign, don't we, Sam?"

"Sure, Dad. That would be cool. One of our neighbors had that other guy's sign in his yard. I saw it today."

"When we leave here, we'll go get one of John's signs and put it up. Can't let the neighbors have all the fun, can we?"

Sam giggled. "Nope."

Eric took a sip of iced tea and asked the question he was half dreading the answer to but had to know. "Have you made up your mind about moving back, Laci?"

"Not yet. I'm going to call Myra and see if she's interested in taking over the business in Dallas. I need to know that before I can decide about the house."

"I understand. I'm sure it's a hard decision to make."

"It is. And I want to do what the Lord wants me to do. I just haven't had a clear answer about it yet." Laci smiled and added, "I need to pray for patience while I'm waiting, too."

"I'll pray for you, Lace! I been praying you'll stay here."

"You have?"

The smile Laci gave his son squeezed at Eric's heart. He wasn't about to tell her yet, but he'd been praying the very same thing for the last few days.

Sam nodded. "Yes. Dad says I have to remember that what I want may not be God's will, and I know that. But I sure am hoping it is. And I'm praying real hard."

Eric needed the reminder, too.

"Thank you, Sam." Laci reached out and ruffled his hair. "That means a lot to me."

ها

When they left the diner, Laci went one way and the Mitchells another. Sam was excited about seeing a real campaign office. Eric told her he'd let her know if he was able to work Richard into any conversation he had with John.

Laci went home and put in a load of wash then sat down at the kitchen table and dialed Myra's cell phone number. She picked up on the second ring.

"Myra, it's Laci. Can you talk, or are you with a client?"

"I'm at home, but I'm meeting a new client at the shop this afternoon. I was going to call you later today and see how things are. How is your grandmother doing?"

"She's steadily improving. We think she'll be able to get rid of her cane in a week or so."

"That's wonderful, Laci! And I have more good news for you."

"Oh? I'm always ready for good news."

"Well, we've gained three new clients just in the last week. I wanted to be sure about them before I called or e-mailed you. The jobs are pretty substantial. One kitchen remodel and one bedroom redecoration, and the one I'm meeting with today wants her whole upstairs redone."

"Wow, Myra! You've been working hard!"

"No, it's just time. Word gets around from some satisfied clients, and while it takes time, the business grows. I think you'll find this is going to be a very good year for Little Touches."

Was the Lord trying to tell her something? Laci didn't know. Maybe He wanted to find out if she really wanted to stay here or return to Dallas with business getting better.

But Laci didn't feel the urge to rush back just because business had picked up. She just felt she needed to get Myra to hire someone to help her. Praying that Myra's response to her question would give her the answer she needed, Laci took a deep breath.

"Myra, how would you like to own your own business?"

twelve

Laci still didn't have any definitive answers about what to do after talking to Myra. She'd taken her friend by surprise, and Myra said she needed some time to think about it. She suggested Laci let things go on as they had been with her managing things in Dallas and hiring some extra help so Laci didn't feel she had to decide right away.

"It's a big decision, Laci. And it might be colored by your grandmother's close brush with death," Myra had said. "Think about it, and pray about it—and so will I. I'm sure the Lord will give us both the right answers."

Oddly enough, even though no decision had been reached, Laci felt at peace after the phone call. She had faith the Lord would guide her in making the right choice.

The next day was Sunday, and her parents invited everyone out to their ranch after church. She was glad that once again Eric and Sam were included.

"I hope you don't mind, Laci. I'm not trying to matchmake here, but I wanted to invite Eric and his son after seeing how much they enjoyed being at Sara and Jake's that day. And then I saw the way Sam came running up to you after church today." Her mother shrugged as she sliced tomatoes for the hamburgers Laci's dad was grilling. "I just had to ask them."

"It's okay, Mom," Laci said, wondering why everyone was willing to matchmake for the rest of the family but not for her. She fought off sudden tears while she sliced an onion. "Sam heard you tell me about it, and I'd have been worrying about the two of them if you hadn't asked them."

Her mother looked at her closely. "Laci, honey, are you crying?"

"I'm cutting onions, Mom," Laci said, using them as an excuse but not sure they were the whole reason.

"Oh, that's right. I didn't realize they were so strong, dear."

"It's all right." Laci didn't know why she felt so weepy today. Sam had touched her heart when he'd run up to her at church and hugged her. And just the thought of him and Eric spending the afternoon alone had made her heart twist in pain. It was then she knew without a doubt she loved the little boy and. . . was falling more and more in love with his dad each day. But Eric had given her no reason to believe he felt the same way, and maybe that was what had suddenly brought on the tears.

How could she move here and open herself up to being hurt? But, on the other hand, how could she return to Dallas and turn her back on the possibility of a lifetime of happiness here?

Laci took a deep breath and slowly let it out. Patience. She had to have patience. The Lord would guide her. He would. By the time the rest of the family and Eric and Sam arrived, Laci had her tears under control.

Sam seemed in his element around her family, and Meggie appeared to enjoy his company, too. The homemade play set she, John, Jake, and Luke had grown up using was still as sturdy as it ever had been, and the children spent the major part of the afternoon swinging, sliding, and climbing all over it.

But the peaceful afternoon suddenly came to a halt when the women were cleaning up after the meal. Her mother had used paper plates and plastic cups and utensils, but several things still needed to be washed and put away. Sara had just turned from putting the leftover onions in the refrigerator when she stopped and bent over, moaning.

"Rae, go get Jake and Michael, please," Aunt Nora said. "Sara hasn't been feeling well all morning. I think it's time."

"I'm—not sure—" Sara tried to say, but another pain hit before she could finish. Rae hurried outside.

"Well, unless you want to have that baby right here in Lydia's kitchen, we need to get Michael's opinion and let your husband know you are in labor."

In minutes the two men ran into the kitchen. After talking to Sara and watching her as another wave of pain seemed to wash over her, Michael said, "I'd get her to the hospital as soon as I could if I were you, Jake."

"We're on our way. Will you two take care of Meggie, Aunt Nora?" Jake asked as he helped Sara to the door.

"You know we will. We'll probably be right behind you."

"We're going out the front so Meggie doesn't get scared."

Laci's mom shooed at them. "Go. We'll take care of everything here. And we'll probably all be there before the baby gets here."

Excitement grew as they told everyone else a new member of the family was about to be born. Laci's dad led a prayer that Sara would deliver a healthy baby and be fine. Then everyone loaded into their vehicles and headed for town.

Laci wasn't sure how she ended up riding with Eric and Sam, but they seemed as excited as the rest of the family. By the time they all arrived at the hospital, Sara and Jake were in the delivery room.

For the next few hours they all paced back and forth in the family waiting room. Named after Sara's grandpa and Jake's favorite uncle, William Benjamin Breland was born at six o'clock that evening. He had his mother's blond hair and blue eyes and dimples just like his dad.

Everything took a backseat to baby Ben during the next week as he was welcomed into the family. The women made plans to take turns carrying in meals to Sara and Jake and Meggie, but it was only an excuse to hold the baby while the others ate.

He truly was adorable, and Laci quickly came to love the feel of the little bundle in her arms. He made the sweetest cooing noises, and that little thumb he kept flopping in his mouth fascinated her.

Meggie was precious with her little brother, and for the moment Laci saw no sign of sibling rivalry. It seemed that Jake and Sara had prepared her well. Maybe it was because they made sure she had plenty of attention, too. Wanting to help assure the little girl she was as important to the family as always, Laci took Meggie along with her and Gram and Will to see Sam's game on Tuesday afternoon. Then they joined Eric and Sam at the diner for supper before taking Meggie home.

"How's that new baby doing?" Dee asked after she'd taken their orders and given Meggie and Sam their sheets to color. "John says he looks just like Jake. . .with Sara's hair."

"That's a pretty apt description," Gram said.

"He says he's almost as pretty as Meggie was when she was born," Dee said, smiling at the little girl. "I need to get over there soon and see him."

"He's pwetty cute," Meggie said before she began coloring.

"I wish I had a little brother," Sam said to her. "I'd teach him to play T-ball."

"You can teach Ben when he gets big like you," Meggie said.

"Okay, I will," Sam promised.

Dee grinned. "They sound like miniature adults, don't they?"

"A little bit," Laci said.

It was only after Dee left the table and the children were talking to each other that adult conversation got around to John again. "It sounds as if John is still spending a lot of time here," Gram said.

"It appears that way," Laci said. John had cancelled a few campaign appearances to stay in town and manage the law office so Jake could help Sara with the new baby.

"When I saw John the other day I had a chance to mention seeing Richard talking to Dee at the diner," Eric said. "He didn't seem to like my asking if something was going on between the two of them."

"I'm sure he didn't."

"In fact, he got a little testy about it. I have a feeling John has been spending more time in here since then—"

"It looks like you're right," Will said, as the bell over the diner door jingled and John walked in. He grinned when he saw them and headed over toward their table.

"Hi, everyone. How is that new baby brother doing, Meggie?" John ruffled her hair before pulling up a chair at the end of the table.

"He's good. 'Cept he cwies sometimes. But Mama feeds him, and then he's okay."

"Well, sometimes when I'm real hungry I feel like crying."

Meggie just nodded as if she understood. "Me, too."

That brought a chuckle from the adults.

Dee brought their orders out and asked John what he wanted. Laci tried hard not to notice the special smile John seemed to save only for Dee as he gave her his order. But it was hard to miss. Still, she wasn't going to say a word about it. Not after the other day.

But that smile of John's disappeared quickly when Richard

Tyler came in and sat at the counter. Trying not to let John know there wasn't an adult at their table who wasn't watching for his reaction to the turn of events, Laci asked, "When are you going back out on the campaign trail, John?"

"Huh? Oh." John seemed to be having trouble pulling his gaze away from the sight of Dee waiting on Richard. "I'll probably be gone for a night or two next week."

"How's it going?" Will asked.

"Going? What?" Dee disappeared into the kitchen, and John seemed to relax as he turned his attention back on his family. "Oh, it seems to be going real well. I'm getting pretty good turnouts at all the rallies."

Conversation went on as usual while Dee was in the kitchen or waiting on tables, but when she was up near the counter they had to wait twice as long for John to answer a question or join in the conversation. All in all it was a pretty interesting evening. It was only after Richard left the diner that John seemed to settle down and finally enjoy his meal. But Laci was pretty sure he knew right where Dee was at any given moment.

Just as they were finishing up eating, his cell phone rang. John excused himself to take the call. "Something has come up at campaign headquarters, and I need to get over there for a while. I'll see you all later."

He went to the counter and paid for his meal, but it took him a little longer to leave the cash register than it had to leave their table.

Eric ordered ice cream for Sam and Meggie, but before it arrived at the table Gram yawned. She appeared a little drained, and Will suggested he ought to get her home.

"I am a little tired. I guess it's all the excitement of planning our wedding and now the new baby in the family. Not to mention all this business with John and Dee. Eric, would you mind seeing Laci and Meggie home?"

"Not at all," Eric assured her. "I'd be glad to see these two ladies home this evening."

Laci almost said they'd leave then so Eric didn't have to go out of his way. But Dee had just brought the ice cream to the children, and she saw no reason to ruin their fun. Besides, she wouldn't complain about spending a little more time with Eric and his son.

While Sam and Meggie enjoyed their treats, Laci and Eric talked quietly between themselves. "Sam was thrilled you all came to the game, Laci. I tried to tell him that with a new baby in the family you might be helping out and not make the game."

"I didn't want to miss it. I—Sam has become special to me." How did she tell Eric something about his son had her wanting to call him her own? Or that something about *him* had her wanting the very same thing.

"And you've become special to him. . .and to me. I can't thank you enough for being so good to him."

"Sam is easy to be nice to," Laci said. But her heart twisted in her chest, and she didn't know if it was from joy or pain. It thrilled her to hear she was special to Eric—but in what way? Was it only because of Sam? Oh, she hoped not. She truly hoped not.

જ

When they took Meggie home, Jake and Sara insisted they come in for a while and visit. Baby Ben was asleep, but they got to see him for a few minutes, and then Meggie had to show Sam her toys. Before long they were putting puzzles together in the middle of the floor while the adults talked over coffee in the kitchen.

Laci and Eric told them about John's reaction to Richard Tyler, and Jake began to chuckle.

"Well, I sure don't think Dee is interested in Richard, but he certainly would like for that to change. It won't hurt John to know someone else is interested in Dee. In fact, it may be the *only* thing that spurs him to action."

"Does anyone know what is keeping them apart now?" Laci asked.

Jake shook his head. "Not really. I have an idea, but I don't know for sure. I think they are just afraid of being hurt."

"Well, no one wants to be hurt, but this has been going on for a while now. Do you think maybe they just like wondering how the other feels and hoping it's the same way they do?"

"How could anyone enjoy that, Sara? I mean maybe for a little while, but then—" Laci couldn't imagine wanting to play that kind of guessing game for long. At the moment she was finding it hard to deal with wondering in what way Eric "cared" about her.

"I don't know." Sara shook her head. "I just can't figure those two out."

"Well, I'm about ready to talk to that cousin of mine about it. He needs to know the whole town can see they belong together, and it's about time they admit it."

"Maybe that's the whole thing. Maybe they're afraid of making a commitment. Or maybe Dee is afraid of being a senator's wife."

Sara and Laci looked at each other. That could be it. Laci began to nod her head. "Maybe she is. That would be very daunting for a lot of women. Or maybe she doesn't want to give up her business to move to Washington, D.C., if he wins."

"She wouldn't have to give up the business. She'd just need to hire someone to run it for her."

"Ladies, we could *maybe* this to death," Jake said. "But the truth is, we don't know. It's that simple."

"You are absolutely right, Jake," Sara said. "But, if John ever found out how much fun we're having trying to figure the two of them out, he might take action."

"Maybe it's time we let him know," Jake said, looking over at Laci. "You're his sister. Why don't you see what you can find out?"

"Ha! Not me," Laci said. "I've already given it a shot. He's not going to tell me anything."

"You know. . .maybe it's about time we asked Gram to help out those two," Jake suggested.

"That might be your best idea yet, Jake," Eric said

It was getting late by the time they called it a night and headed toward Gram's. Sam was yawning in the backseat. "I sure had a good time tonight. I like your family, Lace."

"Thanks, Sam. I like yours, too." The words were out of her mouth before she could stop them.

"Mine's just me and Dad."

"I know." Laci hoped she hadn't given herself away—at least not yet. And then it dawned on her that way of thinking could lead to the same kind of game John and Dee were playing. Say a little, but not too much. Wonder and hope, but don't ask. Who was she to put her brother and Dee down when she certainly couldn't imagine just coming out and telling Eric she was in love with him? She prayed silently, *Dear Lord, please help my brother and Dee. Of course they're afraid of being hurt. Who isn't? But, Lord, I don't want to go on for years in limbo like they seem to be doing. And I hope they decide to let each other know how they feel very soon. Please guide me. . . and please guide them. Thank You for Your help.*

Sam was asleep when Eric pulled up at her grandmother's

house. When Eric got out to walk her to the door, Laci said, "You don't need to see me to the door. Gram is still up, and Sam needs to be put to bed."

But Eric walked around the front of the truck anyway. "I'll at least watch you until you go inside then."

"Okay."

But as she climbed out of the truck Eric reached out and touched her on the arm, turning her toward him. "Laci, I'd like to thank you again for coming to Sam's game and for. . . making him feel as if he has family here in Sweet Springs."

"You don't need to thank—"

She was stopped by the touch of his fingertips on her lips.

"Yes, I do," Eric said as he bent his head toward hers. "Just say 'You're welcome, Eric.' That's all," he whispered right before his lips touched hers.

His lips pressed gently against hers, and as he gathered her in his arms Laci found herself kissing him back. She wasn't sure who pulled away first, but it was Eric who said, "Thank you again, Laci."

"Th—" Laci began.

"Uh-uh." Eric's fingertips touched her lips once more, and he shook his head. "Just say—"

She could feel the corners of her mouth turn up. "You're welcome, Eric."

Eric smiled back and nodded before turning to climb into the truck.

Laci hurried up the walk but turned around and waved from the porch before opening the door. Eric waved back and drove off. Laci closed the door and leaned against it for a moment, taking a deep breath. Well, she was more confused than ever. And more in love than she thought she could be. Maybe his talk about families and moving closer wasn't all about her family, after all. Maybe he did care about her and want her to stay here for his and Sam's sake.

But even if Eric cared for her the way she cared for him—there was still Sam to consider. As much as she loved that little boy, could she be the kind of mother he needed—*if* Eric felt the same way about her? And that was a big if. That kiss didn't prove anything. He'd said, "Thank you." Maybe he was still thanking her for being sweet to Sam and not for the kiss. Laci rubbed her suddenly aching temple. How *did* one know?

thirteen

Laci found Gram in the kitchen, puttering around as best she could with the use of her cane. But she seemed to be feeling better than when she'd left the diner.

"Did you get a second wind, Gram?" Laci asked as she took a seat at the table.

"I must have. I took a shower, and that revived me. But I wanted a cup of tea before I went to bed. Would you like one?"

"No, thank you. But let me bring that cup to the table for you." She stood and brought her grandmother's tea to the table.

Gram followed and sat down across from Laci. "Did you and Eric and the kids have a good time?"

Oh, yes, she did. "We did. We visited with Jake and Sara for a while when we got to their house."

Gram nodded. "I know. Jake called me a little while ago. He said you all think I should talk to John."

After the events of the evening Laci took pity on her brother. "Oh, I don't know. He probably can't help it if he doesn't know what to do about Dee."

"Oh? Why do you think that?"

"Well, because. . .all this caring stuff can certainly get confusing at times."

"Yes, it can." Gram blew on the hot tea before taking a sip.

"I mean it's hard to admit you care about someone when you don't know how they feel about you." Laci knew she was talking as much about herself as she was her brother.

Gram looked at her closely then asked bluntly, "Laci, are you falling in love with Eric Mitchell?"

Laci was almost relieved to be able to tell someone. "I think I'm already there, Gram."

"Why, honey, that's nothing to sound so forlorn about. Eric is a wonderful Christian man and a great dad. I'm sure he'll make a terrific husband."

"Whoa, Gram. I said I thought I was in love with Eric. I'm not sure how he feels about me. And for the first time I have an inkling of how confused John might feel about Dee. But for me there's even more to consider. Even if Eric fell in love with me, there's Sam. The thought of a ready-made family scares me, Gram. I know absolutely nothing about being a mom."

"Oh, Laci, honey, you know more than you think you do. You've had a wonderful role model in your own mother. And I've watched you with Sam—and with Meggie and baby Ben for that matter. You're a loving, caring woman. The Lord has given you all the instincts you need, and He will guide you to be a wonderful mother."

"But I don't know how Eric feels about me." She knew how she hoped he felt but still. . .

"Laci, I haven't lived this long without learning a thing or two. I've watched the two of you together, and I've seen how Eric looks at you. For what it's worth, there's not a doubt in my mind he cares about you."

"Thanks, Gram. I hope you're right. But I guess only time will tell." She just prayed it wouldn't take forever to find out. And even if he did care as Gram believed, the thought of becoming an instant mom still had Laci worried. Sam was much too precious a child for her to mess him up.

"Well, you have some time. But I think it's running out for

John and Dee. Someone needs to talk those two into getting their feelings out in the open. I guess that someone might be me. But I have to find out the right way to go about it. I'll take it to the Lord. He'll help me out."

Laci nodded. She had been trying to do that, too. She sure hoped He gave her some answers soon.

ॐ

The next morning Laci still felt as confused as ever. The more she thought about it, the more she began to think the kiss had just been Eric's way of thanking her for her attention to Sam.

And Sam was the one she was concentrating on today. It was much easier to think about him than reflect on the kiss his dad had given her. Thinking about that just made Laci wish for a repeat.

Sam was another matter. He didn't need silly grown-up games in his life. He could be the one who was hurt by it all. And that was the last thing Laci wanted to do. She would continue to go to his games because she'd promised him she would. But other than that it might be time to distance herself from him and his dad a little bit.

But all of that was much easier said than done. When Sam came up to her that night after Wednesday evening Bible study and asked if he could sit with her when everyone gathered in the auditorium for the devotional and singing afterward, she couldn't tell him no. She felt a little uncomfortable when Eric came and sat down on the other side of her; but after the service he acted the same as always, and she tried to do the same. She didn't know whether to be relieved or disappointed he didn't act differently.

The kiss wasn't mentioned, but of course she didn't expect it to be—not with Sam listening to their conversation.

"Lace, we have a tournament this Saturday, and we play

three games during the day. Can you come?" Sam asked.

There was no way she could turn him down. Not when she could tell from the expression on his face how important it was to him. "I'll be there."

"Oh, good. I told Larry you'd come to cheer us on."

"I sure will."

"Thanks, Lace!" Satisfied she'd be there, he ran off to play with some of the other children.

Eric turned to her. "Laci, that will make for a real long day for you. You don't have to come to all three games. It's mostly so the little ones feel part of the bigger league. You know we don't keep score and—"

"Eric, it's important to Sam to have someone to cheer for him whether scores are kept or not. I'll be there."

"Thank you. Again." Eric gave her a slow smile, and only then did Laci have a pretty good idea he hadn't forgotten the kiss anymore than she had.

"You're welcome." She smiled back, but she could feel color flood her face, just remembering the night before. Flustered and not knowing what to say next, she opted for running. "I guess I'd better go find Gram. She's probably ready to go home."

" 'Night then. See you Saturday."

"Okay. Good night." As she hurried off to find her grandmother, she tried to shore up her resolve to put a little distance between herself and the Mitchell men. She'd go to Sam's games as promised, but she had to draw the line there.

Laci found her resolve disappearing, though, when Eric called her later that night. Her pulse started racing the minute she heard his voice on the other end of the line.

"Laci?"

"Hello, Eric. What can I do for you?"

"Well, I've been wanting to thank you for being so sweet to Sam and—"

"Eric, you don't have to thank me or pay me back. I—" She certainly didn't want him feeling he owed her anything.

"I know that. But. . .I'd like to take you to Los Hacienda tomorrow evening. I don't know if you've been there yet, but it's a great Mexican restaurant between Sweet Springs and Ruidoso. It overlooks the Hondo River."

Against her better judgment Laci found she couldn't resist. "It sounds wonderful. I'd love to go."

"Great. I'll pick you up at seven."

"I'll see you then."

Laci hung up the receiver with a shaking hand. So much for her resolve to keep her distance.

"Who was that, dear?" her grandmother asked.

"It was Eric. He asked me to go to a Mexican restaurant called Los Hacienda." She expected her grandmother to comment about her and Eric, but she didn't.

All she said was, "Oh, you'll enjoy that. It's a very nice restaurant."

❧

When Eric picked her up the next evening, Laci felt like a high school girl going out on her first date.

"You look lovely," he said when she let him in the door.

Laci's heartbeat took off, beating double time at his compliment. She hoped so. She'd bought a new dress for the occasion. It was a teal green sundress with a matching jacket. Up here near the mountains it cooled down at night even in late summer.

"Thank you." Laci thought he looked pretty good himself, dressed in black slacks and a crisp white dress shirt.

They said good night to her grandmother, who was waiting

for Will to pick her up for dinner, and then headed out the door.

"Who is watching Sam tonight?" Laci asked as Eric opened the truck door for her.

"My neighbor's teenage daughter, Amanda. Sam likes her a lot, and I know her mom is next door, so it should be all right."

"I'm sure it will be. Sam is a wonderful little boy. I'm sure he's easy to sit with."

Eric grinned at her. "Thanks for the assurance. I haven't left him much."

Laci hoped that meant he didn't date a lot. As they drove out onto Highway 380, in the close quarters of Eric's truck, she wasn't quite sure how to act. She didn't know if this was a date as she wished or just a thank-you as he'd implied. All she knew was there was no place she'd rather be than here with him.

It took only about fifteen minutes to get to the restaurant, and it more than lived up to her expectations. It was a large hacienda with a beautiful courtyard that overlooked the Hondo River. It was such a beautiful evening that Eric asked if they could be seated outside.

The waiter led them to a table with the view of the river below and handed them menus.

"Oh, this is so nice," Laci said, taking in the surroundings.

"I'm glad you like it. It's my favorite restaurant although I haven't been here in a while."

The night felt even more special at his words. The waiter brought them water and some chips and queso dip while they looked over the menu. Eric recommended the Santa Fe, a combination plate of enchiladas, chile rellenos, and a taco with beans and rice.

"I'm not sure I can eat all of that," Laci said.

"You don't have to. But it's a way to try some of the best in New Mexico."

"It does sound good." She smiled over at him. "I'll have it then."

Once the waiter took their order they were left alone, and it felt romantic to be watching the sunset with Eric. The sky was gorgeous with the shades of mauve, orange, pink, and yellow and a hint of blue green. "I never fail to be awed by the sunsets out here."

"No, neither do I," Eric said.

Laci was a little surprised at how easily their conversation flowed as they waited for their food. They talked about her family and how close it was, about Dee and John and John's chances of being elected in the fall.

"I think he's going to be the next United States Senator from New Mexico," Eric said.

"I certainly hope so."

"He's got my vote, that's for sure. He'll do his best for the state and keep his integrity."

"He will do that." Laci had every confidence in her brother.

The waiter brought their dinners, and the conversation turned to Sweet Springs and New Mexico and how varied its scenery was.

"I'm glad you came with me tonight, Laci. I've wanted to show you this place for a while now. I love it here."

"It is truly a beautiful restaurant."

Eric nodded. "It is, but that's not what I'm talking about. Not the restaurant, but the area. I've been thinking of building a home up here."

"Really? Where would you put it?"

Eric stood. "Come here. I'll show you."

They walked a little closer to the four-foot wall around the open part of the courtyard, and she had to stand near Eric to see where he was pointing. "Over there, across the river. I'd like to buy a piece of property like that and build a hacienda-style home on it."

It was a gorgeous setting, with the sun disappearing in the west and lights on in the distance where daylight turned to twilight in the east.

"Oh, that would be a beautiful place for a home." Laci turned to find Eric's gaze on her, and the expression in his eyes had her heart doing funny little flutters. For a minute she thought he might kiss her, and she truly wished he would. Then the waiter seated a couple at a nearby table, and the moment was lost.

"Maybe one day I'll build up here," Eric said as he led her back to the table.

As she thought of a home in that setting, Laci longed for more than returning to live in this part of the country. But she pushed it to the back of her mind as Eric pulled her chair out for her. "I can see how you would want to live here. And it's not so far away that you couldn't still work in Sweet Springs."

"That's true." He took his seat across from her. "I could work in Ruidoso, too. But for now I'll stay where I am."

Laci nodded. "Sweet Springs is a great place to live and raise a child."

"It is," Eric said, looking thoughtful.

The waiter came and lit the candle on their table. They continued to talk as they watched the evening darken and the sky fill with stars. The more they talked, the more they found they had in common. They both loved old movies and, of course, Mexican food. But they also enjoyed reading and had several books by the same authors. They liked the outdoors, and both loved to ski.

When Eric told her of his worries about raising Sam alone, Laci was more than a little pleased he felt he could confide in her.

"I never realized how much a child needed both parents until I was the only one Sam had left," he said. "After Joni died, well, it took awhile for me to get over that and realize I had to be strong for Sam's sake. I was all he had. Sometimes I feel pretty overwhelmed, though. There are days when I don't have a clue what I'm doing or if I'm doing it right."

"You've done an excellent job of raising Sam, Eric. It can't have been easy."

He shook his head. "No, it hasn't been. But the Lord blessed me with a good little boy. And He helps me every step of the way."

Her feelings for Eric soared at seeing his strong faith in the Lord. "You two are going to be fine."

"Yes, we will. And I'm ready to move on. Sam needs a mother, and I am hoping one day—"

"Well, look who's here," a familiar voice said. "We didn't see you two come in."

They looked up to see Luke and Rae standing there grinning at them. Eric invited the couple to join them, and Laci didn't know whether to be upset or relieved her cousin had interrupted their conversation. Part of her wanted to hear the rest of what Eric was going to say—another part of her was almost afraid to find out what it was.

"Thanks, but we're on our way out," Rae said. "We're going to the movies when we get back to Sweet Springs. We just wanted to stop by and say hello."

Luke and Rae left, and somehow the conversation never returned to where it had been. Was Eric going to say he was ready to find a wife? Even if he was, that "one day" sounded as if he hadn't found a prospect yet, which would mean this was the thank-you dinner Laci hadn't wanted—instead of the date she'd wished for. She sighed inwardly as Eric paid the bill and they headed outside to his truck. She'd been right yesterday. She would *have* to distance herself from the Mitchell men.

❧

Eric didn't know what happened, but after Luke and Rae came to the table things seemed to change. The evening had been perfect until then, and he'd been on the verge of telling Laci one day he hoped she'd care about him the way he cared about her. But after the interruption he didn't know how to bring it up again.

Laci seemed a little quiet on the way back to Sweet Springs, leaving him to wonder what had changed between them. When they arrived back at her grandmother's home, he walked her to the door, hoping to recapture some of the earlier mood.

"Thank you for going with me," he said, looking into her eyes.

"Thank you for asking me. I had a very nice time," Laci said with a smile.

"I'm glad. So did I." Eric wanted to kiss her good night. And if the mood from the restaurant had still been there, he wouldn't have hesitated. But now. . .

"Good night," Laci said, opening the door and slipping inside to look at him through the screen door.

Eric sighed. He'd thought too long, and his chance was gone.

"Good night, Laci." He smiled and gave her a little salute. He headed for his truck determined to act more quickly the next time. And then he prayed there would be a next time.

Laci's plans to distance herself from Sam and Eric seemed to be disintegrating before her eyes. The love and pride she felt for the little boy grew each time he looked up into the stands to see her cheering for him after he'd made a home run on Saturday.

After Sam's team won its third game that day, she and the part of her family that had been able to make it to the game were telling him and Eric good-bye. It was then Laci knew she couldn't turn her back on Sam.

He threw his arms around her and said, "Thanks for coming, Lace." And then out of nowhere he added, "I love you."

Those three little words shot straight into Laci's heart, and she suddenly felt she knew what the Lord wanted her to do. She hugged him back and said, "I love you, too, Sam."

With those words Laci felt the decision to move back to Sweet Springs had been made for her. No matter how things turned out between her and Eric, she was moving back home. If Eric didn't feel the same about her as she did him, she'd just have to trust the Lord to help her handle her feelings for him and deal with the pain. But she wasn't going to turn her back on Sam. She was certain the Lord didn't want her to. And neither did she. She was going to be there for Eric's child as long as he needed her to be.

fourteen

Laci called Myra as soon as she got home from the ball field that afternoon and told her of her decision. She realized the Lord would be working in Myra's life as He was in her own. So she left the decision up to Myra as to whether she would buy out her interest in Dallas or just manage it for her.

"I was hoping you would call, Laci. And I'm not surprised at all about what you've decided. If I didn't already live around them, I'd have made the same decision to be closer to family—as my sweet husband has pointed out to me. And we've talked things over. I'd like to buy out your interest in this shop if that's the way you're leaning. And I'm very willing to change the name so you can keep Little Touches as yours."

Laci breathed a sigh of relief. That was the decision she was hoping for. She didn't want to start a chain of shops. She just wanted one, right here in her hometown. "That is wonderful news, Myra. I'll get in touch with Jared Morrison, the lawyer who helped me get the shop up and running, and let him handle the sale for us, if that's all right with you."

"It's fine."

"Okay then. I'll contact him next week and get back to you. I'll have to come back to sign the papers and move things out of my apartment, so I'm comforted we'll be seeing each other. But just know I wish you the very best, Myra."

"You know I wish the same for you, Laci. I'll talk to you soon."

Laci hung up the telephone feeling as if one chapter of her

life had ended and another begun. She didn't know what the future held for her. All she knew was she would try to place it in the Lord's hands.

"Laci? Can you come downstairs, dear?" Gram called from below.

"I'll be right there." Laci felt like a kid taking the stairs two at a time.

"What can I do for you, Gram?" she asked, finding her at the kitchen table with a tablet and pen in hand.

"I've decided to have a Sunday night supper tomorrow night if you'll help, Laci," Gram said. "I know it's short notice, but I've been missing them a lot. And, besides, I've figured out that may be the way to get John and Dee together before he goes out on the campaign trail again."

"Oh? How do you think you'll manage that with everyone around?"

"Don't you worry about it." Gram grinned. "I'm not telling because I don't want anyone giving away my plans. And this isn't going to be my normal Sunday night supper for the whole church. Since the doctor hasn't released me to do things as usual, it'll be more like a trial run before the real thing. This time it's just going to be the family and David and Gina and a few others from church."

"Okay. That's probably best since you still need your cane and tire a little easier. But I'll do most of it, Gram. You only need to tell me what you want me to do."

"That's what I was hoping you'd say." Gram handed Laci a piece of paper. "I've sent Will to the store for the biggest ham he can find. If you'll help me line up the family to bring food and call the others on this list, we'll see what happens."

"What about John and Dee? Are you sure you can get them both here?"

"I've already made a point of asking Dee to be here, and she said she wouldn't miss it. And John thinks it's partly a send-off for his next round of campaigning so he'll be here."

By ten that night everyone was invited, and the food was planned. Laci was going to put the huge ham Will had brought from the grocery in the oven the next morning and bake several cakes after they returned home from church. Everyone else would bring different sides and a few more desserts.

Laci could barely wait until the next day to see what Gram had up her sleeve. Plus, Eric and Sam were on the list, and she was looking forward to seeing them somewhere besides church, the diner, or the ball field. Only when she was getting ready for bed that night did she realize she hadn't told anyone her news about staying here. But that was okay. They'd find out soon enough.

ও

Eric couldn't help but notice something was different about Laci the next day at church. When Sam hurried up to her, she seemed more open and less guarded with him, and she looked. . .more relaxed and at ease than he'd ever seen her.

"Hi, Lace! Can I sit with you today? Dad said we're coming over to your house for supper after church tonight."

"Yes, you are! It's going to be fun." Laci hugged him. "And I'd love for you to sit with me."

His son seemed to have a way with Laci that Eric wished he could emulate. But her openness with his son didn't seem to carry over to him, and Eric wasn't quite sure how to deal with it.

At first he'd been afraid he might have damaged their relationship by kissing her the night he'd taken her home from Jake and Sara's. But then she'd agreed to go to Los Hacienda with him on Friday, and things had seemed to be going well for a while. But after Luke and Rae had stopped by their table something seemed to change.

Since then he'd been doing a lot of thinking and had come to the conclusion he and Laci weren't that much different from John and Dee. Neither one knew how the other felt except that they *cared*. But did she care about him just because he was Sam's dad? Or did she care about him as a man? And had he let her know he was in love with her? No.

Well, the next time he kissed her he wanted Laci to know without a doubt that he was telling her he loved her. But how would he ever get to that point? He didn't know. When the service was over he didn't even have a chance to start up a conversation.

"I have to hurry home to help Gram set up for tonight, but I'll see you both later, okay?" Laci said, but it was Sam she was smiling at and not Eric.

"We'll be there," Eric answered, wishing she would look at him. But she hurried off with a wave and left Eric more determined than ever to find a way to talk to her. Soon.

"I can't wait until tonight, Dad," Sam said.

"Neither can I, son. Neither can I."

❧

Laci was too busy that afternoon to be nervous about seeing Eric again that night. Knowing he would be there, however, added an extra dollop of anticipation for the evening. Not that she didn't have enough already, wondering what Gram had up her sleeve concerning Dee and John.

By the time everyone started arriving at Gram's after church that evening, the whole family seemed to know something was up. Gram had evidently told Jake and Sara she might talk to John tonight, and Jake told Luke and Rae, who in turn told Aunt Nora and Michael. Laci's parents had been the last to know.

"Mom, I hope you know what you're doing," Laci's mom

said when she brought her potato casserole into the kitchen through the back door. "All this could backfire and send Dee and John further apart."

"Well, Lydia, someone has to do something. And in my *condition* he's not likely to react quite as fiercely as he might with any of the rest of you." Gram chuckled. "At least I hope not."

Laci's mother shook her head. "Well, he will take interference from you easier than he will from Ben or me. But you know how private John is."

"I do. Of all my grandchildren he's the one who keeps things to himself the most. But it'll be all right, Lydia. And you don't know what I have planned anyway. Just try not to worry, okay?"

"I'll try not to." She sighed and took her dishes through to the dining room to set them on the table.

Rae came back into the kitchen from depositing her green-bean casserole and a big dish of creamed corn on the dining room table. "Gram, you might want to talk to them right here in this kitchen. It's a special one, and it's the very first place Luke kissed me."

"It is?" Laci asked.

"Yes. I'll never forget that night," Rae said, a dreamy expression on her face.

"What night?" Sara asked as she entered the kitchen with baby Ben in her arms.

"The night Luke kissed me right here in Gram's kitchen. I love this room."

Sara smiled. "I know what you mean. It's where I saw Jake for the first time when he moved back to Sweet Springs."

"I didn't know my kitchen held such romantic memories for the two of you," Gram said with a chuckle.

Neither did Laci. But after hearing Sara and Rae's stories she found herself wishing she could get Eric to come that way.

Dee showed up, and Laci could tell they were trying to act normal around her so as not to make her suspicious. But they didn't pull it off.

"You all seem. . .wound up tonight," she said. "What's up?"

"I think we're all happy to be having a Sunday night supper again," Laci's mother said. "We've missed it."

Well, that was certainly a true statement, Laci thought, even if it did avoid Dee's question. Sara and Rae quickly left the room, saying they would see if everyone was there yet.

"Well, I can tell you I'm excited," Gram said. "I haven't—"

"The girls said you wanted a head count, Ellie," Aunt Nora said, as she swept into the room. "John just drove up, and David and Gina are right behind him. Far as I can tell, everyone you invited is here."

"Good," Gram said, taking off her apron and leading the others to the dining room. "I'll have David say a blessing, and we can get started."

Gram hadn't given anyone an idea of how she planned to get John and Dee together, and Laci was almost too nervous to eat, waiting to see. She spotted Gram whispering to Will, and he grinned and nodded his head.

Then David began his prayer, and Laci and the others bowed their heads.

"Dear Lord, we thank You for this family and these friends who have gathered together tonight. We thank You that Ellie has recuperated enough to feel up to having us all here once more. We ask You to bless this food for the nourishment of our bodies, and we thank You above all for Your plan for our salvation through Your Son and our Savior, Jesus Christ. It is in His name I pray, amen."

A line formed on both sides of the table, and everyone began helping themselves. Laci found Eric and Sam and offered to help Sam fix his plate. Once he was settled beside Meggie on the bottom step of the staircase and began to eat, Laci and Eric went back to the line and ended up behind John. Laci figured that whatever Gram had planned it wouldn't happen until after they'd eaten.

But then she spotted Aunt Nora saying something to Dee, and Dee nodded and disappeared into the kitchen. A second later Gram motioned for John, and he left the line to see what she wanted. Then *he* disappeared into the kitchen. After a moment Will came out and handed Gram what looked like a key. She grinned, and after a second or two she went back into the kitchen.

It was no more than a minute before everyone heard a banging of some kind coming from the kitchen. And then a loud "Somebody come and unlock this door!"

"That's John," she said to Eric. "I'd know that yell anywhere. Let's find out what Gram's done."

When she and Eric entered the kitchen Gram was standing outside her pantry door grinning, and John was shouting at the top of his lungs, "We're locked in! Someone let us out!"

He banged on the door again while more family members made their way into the kitchen. Before long, even Meggie and Sam had come to see what was going on.

"John, I'm here, and I have the key!" Gram yelled over the noise.

"Oh, good," John said. "Somehow Dee and I got locked in."

"Yes, well, you're going to stay there for a while, too."

"I thought you said you had the key, Gram."

"I do. But I'm not unlocking that door until you and Dee do some talking. This whole family—not to mention half the town—thinks it's about time you two tell each other what we've known for years—that you love each other!"

"Oh, Gram, I can't believe you did this. It's not necessary. Unlock the door, please."

Laci was surprised John didn't sound angry—in fact, it sounded like laughter in his voice.

"Not until you two talk, and you haven't had time to do that yet."

"We've already done all of that, Gram." John chuckled then. "More times than you can imagine."

"We really have, Ellie." Dee's voice was heard through the door.

Gram looked back at the small crowd in the kitchen and raised her eyebrow. "What do you mean?"

"If you unlock this door and let us out, we'll tell you."

Gram looked at the other family members. "What do you think? Should I let them out?"

"Well, I certainly want to hear what they have to say," Laci's mom said.

"I do, too," Jake added. "Go ahead and let them out, Gram."

"Is the whole family in the kitchen, Gram?" John asked.

Gram looked around the room. "Well, yes. Most of them anyway."

"This is without a doubt the most meddling, nosy family a man could have!" John shouted. A second or two passed in silence. "But I guess we need to level with you if we're to have any peace. Please unlock the door, Gram."

"Oh, all right," Gram said, taking the key and unlocking the door.

John threw the door open and led Dee out while the group in the kitchen clapped.

Dee turned a delicate shade of pink, and John just stood there shaking his head. He handed Gram a pack of napkins, and Dee handed her some plastic cups.

"I think these are what you sent us in there for," John said.

Gram took the items and handed them to Will. "Thank you, but I don't need them after all."

"That comes as no surprise to me," John said a bit sarcastically, but he did at least have a smile on his face.

"All right," Gram said. "You've been released. Now it's time to let us in on whatever it is you and Dee have been up to."

"Us! Gram, you're the one—"

Dee placed her hand on John's arm and patted it. "John, you told your grandmother we'd level with them. And quite frankly it will be a relief to get this all out in the open. Keeping things from them has been more of a strain than I thought it would be. Please."

Laci's brother looked at Dee and then pulled her into the crook of his arm. "All right." He cleared his throat and looked out at his family. "This goes back a ways. Some of you know Dee and I dated for a while in high school, but before I went off to college Dee broke up with me, saying she didn't want me to feel tied down while I was there. I tried to convince her I didn't want to date anyone else, but she said I would once I got there."

John looked at Dee again. "But she didn't tell me the whole story. What I didn't know, until years later, was that because she couldn't afford to go to college at the time she somehow had the notion I wouldn't feel the same about her after I'd been around all those college girls. When she wouldn't date me when I came home, I thought she didn't care."

"But I did," Dee said. "I never stopped caring."

John dropped a kiss on the top of her head. "Thank the good Lord for that. But we drifted away from each other. To make a long story short—and I'm not about to tell you *all* the details—when Dee took over ownership of the diner after her mom moved away, we started seeing more of each other. Finally, in the last year—about the time Luke and Rae got together—we realized we still cared deeply about each other. But, with me running for senator and the circus that can be, I was afraid the media would drive Dee away with all their questioning."

A murmur of understanding passed around the room.

"And I didn't want her to think I was asking her to marry me just to help my chances of winning the election, as many have suggested—some even in this family. So we decided to put off announcing our plans to marry until after the election—"

A collective cheer interrupted John at his admission that they planned to get married. He just grinned and shook his head. Once things quieted down, he continued. "You've made it extremely hard on us to keep our feelings a secret because we've known you wanted us to get together for a while now. And I've wanted to shout to the rooftops that Dee and I are engaged. Not to mention how badly I've wanted to tell old Richard to quit flirting with my girl and get out of the diner—especially since some of you have been *so* willing to let me know what he was up to." He shot Jake and Luke and even Eric a look that spoke volumes. "But now you are all in on our secret, and we're expecting you to help us keep it one."

Laci was the first to speak as she stepped over to hug him and Dee. "You big lug. Of course we'll keep it a secret."

Her dad and mom congratulated the couple next, and then the rest of the family did. "I can't think of anyone I'd want for a daughter-in-law more than you, Dee. My son is a lucky man," Laci's mother said as she hugged Dee.

Both tears and laughter filled the room. Finally this couple the whole family had hoped would get together had already found their way there. . .and on their own.

"Ellie, do you think I could borrow some of those bridal magazines after you're through?" Dee asked.

"Of course you can. What fun! We can plan our weddings

together! You know, Nora and Rae had a double wedding. This is just an idea I'm throwing out, but if you and John want to, Will and I would be more than glad to share our day with you—whatever day you'd like."

"Well, I'm going to leave the four of you to figure that one out," Jake said. "Now that this has had a happy ending I'm going to eat. I'm starved."

The family filed out of the kitchen, talking excitedly about how happy they were. Laci tried to figure out why she had such an ache in her heart when she was so thrilled for her brother and Dee.

But when she glanced at Eric and saw his gaze on her, she knew. Unlike John and Dee, who'd fooled them all and known where they were headed for a good while now, her love life was one great big question mark.

⁂

Later, when her mother asked if she could make it home for both weddings, Laci realized she still hadn't let them know her plans.

"It won't matter, Mom. I'll be here for both, no matter how or when they decide to have them."

"You will?" her mother asked, a hopeful look in her eyes.

Laci nodded. "Yes, I'm moving back. Myra is going to buy out my interest in Dallas, and I'm going into business right here in Sweet Springs. But I don't want to take away any excitement from Dee and John's news tonight. I'll tell the rest of the family later."

But she didn't have to. Sam had been standing behind her, evidently waiting to ask her to help him get a piece of chocolate cake, and had heard every word. He ran toward his dad, yelling, "Dad! Dad! Lace is moving back! She's gonna stay in Sweet Springs!"

fifteen

Eric's gaze met Laci's from across the room. She was staying. *Thank You, Lord.* He took a step toward her, but her family surrounded her. So he shared the joy with his son instead.

"Isn't that great news, Dad?"

"It sure is, Sam." Eric picked up his son and hugged him close. He didn't know which of them was happier at that moment, Sam or him. But Eric's heart seemed to beat a tune to the thought that went over and over in his mind. *Laci is staying. Laci is staying.*

And he was going to have a chance to tell her he loved her. If she didn't return his feelings, he'd just trust in the Lord to help him deal with it. With John and Dee's admission that they'd finally gotten together after years of loving each other, Eric was determined he wasn't waiting that long to let Laci know how deeply he loved her. So many years those two had wasted when they could have been together.

He wouldn't let that happen to him and Laci. And besides he had Sam to consider, too. His son loved Laci. If the two grownups he looked up to couldn't figure out how they felt and let each other know, what kind of example was that for Sam?

Tonight was not the time. But soon, very soon, he and Laci would have to talk.

❧

But the next few weeks didn't provide the opportunity he'd hoped for. Oh, Laci came to Sam's last few T-ball games, but she always had to hurry off afterward to run some errand in connection with wedding or shower plans.

The few times he saw her at the diner, she seemed to be just leaving. Or she was only there to pick up Dee so they could go to Roswell or Ruidoso to look for something to do with the weddings.

Eric kept telling himself he didn't need to rush since Laci wouldn't be going back to Dallas to live, but then he would think of all the years that had passed for John and Dee. He couldn't let that be the case with him and Laci. At the moment, though, he had no choice but to bide his time. She was moving back. He'd have his chance.

Even Sam was moping around the house, and Eric knew it was because he missed seeing Laci, too. Finally, early one evening the week after Sam's T-ball games had ended, he called Laci at her grandmother's only to find she was over at Jake and Sara's.

On the pretense of taking Sam to see Meggie and the new baby, Eric decided to pay Jake and Sara—and Laci, he hoped—a visit. But when he arrived he learned she'd just left.

The frustration must have shown on his face because Sara and Jake insisted he stay for supper. He gratefully accepted the invitation. But it wasn't until afterward, while Meggie and Sam were playing in the den, that he confided his true feelings to his two good friends over a cup of coffee. Weeks ago he'd told Jake he was interested, so it didn't come as a surprise to either of them that he'd fallen in love with Laci.

"This family can spot the lovelorn a mile away, Eric, and you've had that look," Jake said with a chuckle. "Sara and I had a feeling you were a goner and have been thinking about ways to get you two together for weeks."

"Well, I hope you have better luck than I have. I can't seem to get two minutes alone with Laci lately. In fact, I'm beginning to wonder if she's avoiding me."

"She could be," Sara said. "But I don't think it's because she doesn't care. I think she's fallen in love with you, too."

"What makes you say that?"

"As Jake says, this family has a knack for that kind of thing." Sara smiled. "And we share our concerns about each other with each other."

"Then what's the problem? Why is she avoiding me?"

"Well. . .I'm pretty certain she loves you and Sam. But I think she's afraid of becoming an instant mom—that she'll mess up somehow. She loves Sam, but I think she's worried she won't be what he needs as a mother. . .and that would mean she wouldn't be what you need in a wife."

"Oh, that's—crazy. We need *her*." But Eric's heart melted. He knew full well the fears and doubts he had when Sam was born and even more after his wife passed away. It wasn't as if they gave out manuals when a child was born. He'd never had any experience in how to be a dad either, but with the Lord's help he felt as if he'd become a fairly good one. He had no doubt about the kind of mom Laci would be to Sam. None at all. For the first time in days Eric began to hope.

"Well, you know as a group this family is good about getting people together. Do you want us to have Gram lock the two of you in her pantry?" Jake asked, smiling.

"No, but if I don't run into her on my own soon, I may change my mind."

"Just let us know. We can swing into action at a moment's notice." Sara chuckled.

"I'll keep that in mind." And he would. It felt good to think he had at least part of Laci's family on his side.

٭

After John and Dee decided they'd share Gram and Will's

wedding day, the next few weeks were among the busiest Laci could remember. She was thankful, though, that the wedding and shower plans took up so many hours of the day. It gave her less time to dwell on Eric and wonder if she'd ever know how he felt about her.

Sam had only a few more games to play, and she managed to make every one. But then she became sad when the twice-weekly chances to spend time with him and his dad disappeared. With John's campaign in full swing and making plans for the weddings, her family hadn't gotten together since Gram's Sunday night supper. Laci was finding that seeing Eric and Sam only for a little while on Sundays or Wednesdays at church wasn't enough.

They seemed to be going in opposite directions each time they saw one another anywhere else. She told herself that if Eric wanted to see her he'd pick up the phone and call or come by. But then she was rarely at home and hadn't encouraged him. She had no doubts, though, about how she felt about him. Absence from him and Sam was definitely making her heart grow fonder.

She continued to pray for guidance in what to do about her feelings for the two Mitchell men and figured the Lord was giving her a lesson in patience. He'd let her know in His time.

Meanwhile she was growing closer to her family. They had all promised to hold John and Dee's engagement a secret and had kept their word. The wedding date had been set for the weekend after the election in November. That would give both couples a chance to enjoy a wedding trip and return home in time to celebrate Thanksgiving with the family.

Laci was glad when Dee promoted Annie to assistant manager so Dee would have free time from the diner to plan her wedding. Deciding to have a double wedding with Gram and Will gave her the opportunity to plan her own without raising suspicions about her and John.

The trips Laci and Dee made to Roswell and Ruidoso looking for dresses enabled Dee to try them on "just for fun." When she found the one she wanted, she'd know what size to order and have it shipped to her instead of bringing it home with her.

Laci was thankful for the busyness during each day, but then at night she wondered what Eric and Sam had done that day. Did they go to the diner for supper or eat at home? Did either one of them miss her half as much as she missed them? She didn't think it was possible. Then she'd take her confusion, doubts, and hopes to the Lord in prayer, trusting that someday she'd have the answers she sought.

※

Eric was beginning to think he would have to ask Jake and Sara for help if he was ever going to tell Laci how he felt. He kept missing her everywhere he went. But he worried he wouldn't know how to tell her how much he loved her and assure her she was the woman he and Sam both wanted and needed.

Then one day a few weeks before the start of school Sam came in from playing. He had missed the cut-off date for turning six since his birthday wasn't until November, so he'd be starting kindergarten this year instead of first grade. And school and its activities were clearly on his mind.

"Dad, who's gonna make cupcakes for me when I need to take them for a party this year?"

"Well, son, I guess I can manage it. I made a cake once."

"It was kind of burnt, Dad."

He remembered it well. "Okay, how about we buy some from the bakery?"

"Do you think Lace might make them for me? She'll be living here then."

"Well, she probably would, son, but—"

"Dad." Sam let out a big sigh. "Why don't you just ask Lace to marry us? You love her, don't you?"

"Yes, son, I do. It's just not that easy."

"Why not?"

"Well. . ." _Why not?_ "Sam, you just gave me an idea. Hang on." He punched in Jake's number. "I need that favor. Can you find out where Laci is going to be for the next thirty minutes?"

Jake chuckled. "I'll do my best."

"Okay. Call me back on my cell phone."

"Will do."

"Come on, son. Get in the truck." Eric grabbed his keys from the counter and led the way outside to his pickup.

"Where are we goin', Dad?" Sam asked as he climbed in and buckled up.

"To find Laci."

&.

Laci and her grandmother were in the kitchen poring over recipes, trying to decide on the best chocolate cake recipe for the groom's cake for Will. John didn't like chocolate so they'd already decided his would be lemon.

"Why don't we make both of these, Gram, and let Will decide which one he likes better? I'm sure it's going to be your chewy chocolate one, though."

"That's probably the best idea. I'm sure Will won't mind the decision-making process one bit."

"No, I don't think so, either." Laci chuckled, knowing how much Will loved cake.

The phone rang, and Gram went to answer it while Laci

was in the pantry gathering the ingredients they'd need. She heard a knock on the back door. "I'll get the door, Gram."

She deposited a box of cocoa, two cake pans, and cooking oil on the counter by the canisters and went to open the door.

Her heart did a nosedive into her stomach when she saw Eric standing there.

"Hi, Eric. Where's Sam? Is something wrong?"

"No. Well, at least I don't think so. Sam just needs to talk to you. Says he needs you. He's in the truck out front."

"Why didn't you bring him in?" Laci asked as she hurried around the corner of the house.

"He wanted me to get you." Eric followed at a slower pace.

True enough, Sam was in the truck. Laci opened the door and asked, "What is it, Sam? What do you need, honey?"

"Oh, Lace! I've been missin' you! I need you to be my mom. *Please* say you'll marry Dad!"

"But I—"

"*Please* say yes, Laci," Eric said from behind her.

Laci looked at Eric and then at Sam. "What? I—"

Eric grinned. "I figured Sam might have a better chance of convincing you to marry me than I would." He turned her to face him and took her hands in his. His gaze caught hers, and she couldn't look away. "I love you, Laci Tanner. We love you. With all of our hearts. And we want nothing more than for you to marry me and become my wife and Sam's mom. . .if you'll have the two of us."

"Oh, Eric. I love you both so much. But I know nothing about being a mother, and I—"

Eric pulled her into his arms and claimed her lips with his, silencing her words. He kissed her fully then, after a long moment, stepped back. "Please just say, 'I'll marry you, Eric.' That's all we want to hear."

Before she could say anything he kissed her again. She knew now. He loved her.

Laci pulled back then. She gazed into Eric's eyes, her lips turning up into a smile. "Yes, I'll marry you, Eric."

"Woo-hoo!" Sam yelled. "Lace is gonna marry us and be my mom!"

epilogue

Mid-November

If Laci thought she was busy before, she found the pace nearly impossible to keep up with after she and Eric announced their engagement. Gram and Will and John and Dee had quickly insisted they share their wedding day with them.

"I've never seen a triple wedding before, but just think how much our guests will love us if they get three weddings out of one outfit," Gram had said, chuckling. "We'll have all our relatives and friends in one spot. We might as well kill three birds with one stone."

It made sense to everyone. The doctor released Gram to resume her normal activities without a cane, and from then on there was a whirlwind of activity in and out of Sweet Springs. After all their trips to Roswell and Ruidoso, Laci and the other women found the wedding outfits they wanted while accompanying Laci to Dallas to sign the papers to her business and pack up her apartment.

Their three dresses were beautiful. Gram's was a gorgeous silver taffeta gown that brought out her silver curls. Dee's gown was an ivory charmeuse slip dress with a lace overlay, and Laci chose a champagne-colored lace and organza gown with a dropped waist. Meggie's dress was ivory organza with tiny rosebuds scattered randomly around the skirt.

They'd had parties to address and stamp invitations and one surprise shower after another. Gram was especially touched by the shower the Teddy Bear Brigade helped with. She'd thought she was planning one for Dee and Laci but found hers had been in the works much longer.

True to everyone's expectations, John was elected the new United States Senator from New Mexico, and he and Dee would be taking up residence in Washington, D.C., in the coming year.

Laci still couldn't believe their wedding day had finally arrived. Gram and Will would go first, then John and Dee, with Laci and Eric's wedding last. They would all walk down the aisle, with Meggie as flower girl and Sam as ring bearer leading the way. Then David, the minister who had married the rest of the family, would perform each ceremony. He'd laughingly accused them of trying to get a group rate.

Laci blinked back tears as she watched her sweet grandmother and Will, and then her brother and Dee, become man and wife. Then finally it was time for her and Eric.

Her heart felt as if it would burst with love while she and Eric said their vows in front of their loved ones. As they shared their first kiss as a married couple, she felt a tug on her wedding gown. Laci looked down to see Sam grinning up at her and his dad. "Now you really are my mom," he said.

"Yes, I really am," Laci assured him.

Eric reached down and lifted Sam up between the two of them, and they turned to the room full of family and friends. Then David announced, "I now present to you, Mr. and Mrs. Eric Mitchell—and son."

Amid laughter and applause Laci and Eric each kissed Sam on the cheek and then, behind his back, shared one more kiss of their very own. Her heart overflowing with love, Laci thanked the Lord for the family He had given her in birth—and now for the family He had given her in marriage.

A Letter To Our Readers

Dear Reader:

In order that we might better contribute to your reading enjoyment, we would appreciate your taking a few minutes to respond to the following questions. We welcome your comments and read each form and letter we receive. When completed, please return to the following:

Fiction Editor
Heartsong Presents
PO Box 719
Uhrichsville, Ohio 44683

1. Did you enjoy reading *Family Reunion* by Janet Lee Barton?
   ❏ Very much! I would like to see more books by this author!
   ❏ Moderately. I would have enjoyed it more if

   _____

   _____

   _____

2. Are you a member of **Heartsong Presents**? ❏ Yes ❏ No
   If no, where did you purchase this book? _____

   _____

3. How would you rate, on a scale from 1 (poor) to 5 (superior), the cover design? _____

4. On a scale from 1 (poor) to 10 (superior), please rate the following elements.

   ____ Heroine   ____ Plot
   ____ Hero   ____ Inspirational theme
   ____ Setting   ____ Secondary characters

5. These characters were special because? _____

_____

_____

6. How has this book inspired your life? _____

_____

_____

7. What settings would you like to see covered in future
   Heartsong Presents books? _____

_____

_____

8. What are some inspirational themes you would like to see
   treated in future books? _____

_____

_____

9. Would you be interested in reading other **Heartsong
   Presents** titles? ❑ Yes ❑ No

10. Please check your age range:
    ❑ Under 18   ❑ 18-24
    ❑ 25-34   ❑ 35-45
    ❑ 46-55   ❑ Over 55

Name _____

Occupation _____

Address _____

City, State, Zip _____

Sugar and Grits

4 stories in 1

*S*outhern hospitality enriches four Mississippi romances.

Houston, Texas, authors DiAnn Mills, Martha Rogers, Janice Thompson, and Kathleen Y'Barbo have used their appreciation of small-town life to create this engaging collection.

Historical, paperback, 352 pages, 5³/₁₆" x 8"

Presents